Biggles thought swif̶... ...ou would like me to be̶... ...the British,' he said blu̶...

The General looke̶... ...but mincing matters, that is precisely what I do mean,' he said gravely. 'Obviously, I cannot detail you for such work, but it is hardly necessary for me to remind you that it is the duty of every Englishman to do his best for his side whatever the sacrifice it may involve. That is why I am asking you to volunteer for what may prove a very difficult and dangerous task.'

Captain W. E. Johns was born in Hertfordshire in 1893. He flew with the Royal Flying Corps in the First World War and made a daring escape from a German prison camp in 1918. Between the wars he edited *Flying* and *Popular Flying* and became a writer for the Ministry of Defence. The first Biggles story, *Biggles the Camels are Coming* was published in 1932, and W. E. Johns went on to write a staggering 102 Biggles titles before his death in 1968.

www.**randomhousechildrens**.co.uk

BIGGLES BOOKS
PUBLISHED IN THIS EDITION

FIRST WORLD WAR:
Biggles Learns to Fly
Biggles Flies East
Biggles the Camels are Coming
Biggles of the Fighter Squadron

SECOND WORLD WAR:
Biggles Defies the Swastika
Biggles Delivers the Goods
Biggles Defends the Desert
Biggles Fails to Return

BIGGLES
flies EAST

CAPTAIN W.E. JOHNS

RED FOX

Red Fox would like to express their grateful thanks
for help given in the preparation of these editions to Jennifer Schofield,
author of *By Jove, Biggles*, Linda Shaughnessy of A. P. Watt Ltd
and especially to the late John Trendler.

BIGGLES FLIES EAST
A RED FOX BOOK 9781782952084

First published in Great Britain by Oxford University Press 1935

This Red Fox edition published 2003

Red Fox Books are published by Random House Children's Publishers UK,
61–63 Uxbridge Road, London W5 5SA
A Random House Group Company

Addresses for companies within The Random House Group Limited
can be found at: www.randomhouse.co.uk/offices.htm

THE RANDOM HOUSE GROUP Limited Reg. No. 954009

A CIP catalogue record for this book is available from the British Library.

The Random House Group Limited supports The Forest Stewardship
Council® (FSC®), the leading international forest-certification organisation.
Our books carrying the FSC label are printed on FSC®-certified paper.
FSC is the only forest-certification scheme supported by the leading
environmental organisations, including Greenpeace. Our
paper procurement policy can be found at
www.randomhouse.co.uk/environment

MIX
Paper from
responsible sources
FSC® C016897

Printed and bound in Great Britain by Clays Ltd, St Ives plc

Contents

	Foreword	7
1	How it Began	11
2	Algy Gets a Shock	22
3	Biggles Gets a Shock	32
4	A Meeting and a Duel	39
5	The New Bullet	51
6	More Shocks	60
7	Still More Shocks	74
8	Forced Down	80
9	A Fight and an Escape	92
10	Shot Down	101
11	A Night Flight	113
12	A New Pilot—and a Mission	123
13	Vickers Versus Spandaus	135
14	Biggles Flies a Bomber	143
15	Ordeal by Night	157
16	Checked	166
17	Hare and Hounds	178
18	An Unwelcome Visitor	187
19	Biggles Gets Busy	199
20	The Night Riders	212
21	Sterne Takes a Hand	223
22	Biggles Explains	232

Foreword

The careers of most of those who served in the Great War* for any length of time resolve themselves, in retrospect, into a number of distinct phases, or episodes, rather than one continuous period of service in the same environment. For example, an artillery officer serving in France might find himself, a month later, acting as an aerial gunner on the Italian Front, and after seeing service in that capacity for a while would be sent home to England to get his pilot's wings. Later, when he qualified, he might be rushed off to fill a vacancy in another theatre of war—possibly Salonika or East Africa.

Each of these periods was quite unlike the others; it represented a different climate, a different set of faces, and an entirely different atmosphere.

The career of Captain James Bigglesworth, M.C., D.F.C. (known to his friends as 'Biggles'), was no exception, as those who have read his already published war experiences will agree. But there was one period that has not so far been mentioned, and the reasons have been twofold.

In the first place Biggles, far from taking any credit for the part he played in this particular affair, regards the whole tour of duty with such distaste that even his

---

* The First World War 1914–18. Principal contenders, the Allies: Britain, France, Russia, Italy, Serbia, Belgium, Japan (1915), Romania (1916), USA (1917). Against the Central Powers: Germany, Austria-Hungary, Turkey and Bulgaria (1915).

friend, the Honourable Algernon Lacey (who, it will be remembered, served with him in No. 266 Squadron when it was stationed at Maranique, in France), seldom if ever referred to it. Just why Biggles should feel this way about what were undoubtedly vital affairs of national importance is hard to see, but the fact remains. Like many other successful air fighters, he was a law unto himself, and intolerant of any attempt to alter his point of view—which may have been one of the reasons why he was successful.

Secondly, the Official Secrets Act* has been tightened up, and as one of the principal actors in the drama that is about to be disclosed was alive until recently—not only alive, but holding an important position in the German Government—it was thought prudent to remain silent on a subject that might have led to embarrassing correspondence and possibly international recriminations. This man, who at the time of the events about to be narrated was a trusted officer of the German Secret Service, in the end met the same fate as those of his enemies who fell in his hands—blindfold, with his back to a wall, facing a firing party in the cold grey light of dawn. Whether or not he deserved his fate is not for us to question.

There is little more to add except that Biggles, at the time, was a war-hardened veteran of twelve months' active service. He had learnt to face the Spandaus** of the German Fokkers without flinching, and the *whoof, whoof, whoof* of 'archie'*** bursting around his machine

---

* Official Secrets Act. An agreement which, when a British subject signs, forbids him or her to disclose confidential information prejudicial to the State.
** German machine-guns were often referred to as Spandaus, due to the fact that many were manufactured at Spandau, Germany.
*** Anti-aircraft gunfire, a Royal Flying Corps expression.

left him unmoved. He afterwards confessed to Algy that it was not until his feet had trodden the age-old sands of the Promised Land that he learnt to know the real meaning of the word Fear.

When he went there he was, like many another air warrior, still a boy; when he came back he was still a boy, but old beyond his years. Into his deep-set hazel eyes, which less than eighteen months before had pondered arithmetic with doubt and algebra with despair, had come a new light; and into his hands, small and delicate—hands that at school had launched paper darts with unerring accuracy—had come a new grip as they closed over joystick and firing lever. When you have read the story perhaps you will understand the reason.

1935   W.E.J.

The word 'Hun' as used in this book, was the common generic term for anything belonging to the enemy. It was used in a familiar sense, rather than derogatory. Witness the fact that in the R.F.C. a hun was also a pupil at a flying training school.

W.E.J

Chapter 1
How it Began

I

Captain James Bigglesworth, R.F.C.*, home from France on ten days' leave, stopped at the corner of Lower Regent Street and glanced at his watch. 'Ten to one; I thought it felt like lunch-time,' he mused, as he turned and strolled in the direction of the Caprice Restaurant, the famous war-time rendezvous of R.F.C. officers in London. At the door he hesitated as a thought occurred to him, and he contemplated dubiously the clothes he was wearing, for he was what would be described in service parlance as 'improperly dressed', in that he was not in uniform but civilian attire. The reason for this was quite a natural one.

His uniform, while passable in Flanders, where mud and oil were accepted as a matter of course, looked distinctly shabby in London's bright spring sunshine, and his first act on arrival had been to visit his tailor's with a view to getting it cleaned and pressed. This, he was informed, would take some hours, so rather than remain indoors he had purchased a ready-made suit of civilian clothes—to wear while his uniform was being reconditioned, as he put it. It was an obvious and pardonable excuse from his point of view, but whether or not it would be accepted by the Assistant Provost

---

* Royal Flying Corps 1914–1918. An army corps responsible for military aeronautics, renamed the Royal Air Force (RAF) when amalgamated with the Royal Naval Air Service on 1 April 1918.

Marshal or the Military Police, if he happened to run into them, was quite another matter. So he hesitated when he reached the fashionable meeting-place, torn between a desire to find someone he knew with whom he could talk 'shop', and a disinclination to risk collision with the A.P.M. and his minions who, as he was well aware, kept a vigilant eye on the Caprice.

'What does it matter, anyway? At the worst they can only cancel my leave, which won't worry me an awful lot,' he decided, and pushed open the swing doors. There were several officers and one or two civilians lounging round the buffet, but a swift scrutiny revealed that they were all strangers, so he selected a small table in a secluded corner and picked up a menu card.

He was still engrossed in the not unpleasant task of choosing his lunch when, out of the corner of his eye, he saw some one appear at his side, and thinking it was only a waiter he paid no immediate attention; but when he became conscious of the fact that some one was in the act of settling in the opposite chair he looked up with surprise and disapproval, for there were plenty of vacant tables.

'Good morning, Captain Brunow,' said the new-comer, easily, and without hesitation.

'Sorry, but you're making a mistake,' replied Biggles curtly, resuming his occupation.

'I think not,' went on the other coolly. 'Have a drink.'

Biggles eyed the speaker coldly. 'No, thanks,' he answered, shortly. 'I have already told you that you are making a mistake. My name isn't Brunow,' he added, in a tone that was calculated to end the conversation forthwith.

'No! Ha, ha, of course not. I quite understand. In the circumstances the sooner a name like that is forgotten the better, eh?'

12

Biggles folded the menu and laid it on the table with deliberation before raising his eyes to meet those of his *vis-à-vis*. 'Are you suggesting that I don't know my own name?' he inquired icily.

The other shrugged his shoulders with an air of bored impatience. 'Don't let us waste time arguing about a matter so trivial,' he protested. 'My purpose is to help you. *My* name, by the way, is Broglace—Ernest Broglace. I—'

'Just a minute, Mr Broglace,' interrupted Biggles. 'You seem to be a very difficult person to convince. I've told you plainly enough that my name is not Brunow. You say yours is Broglace, and, frankly, I believe you, but I see nothing in that to get excited about. As far as I am concerned it can be Dogface, Hogface, or even Frogface. And if, as I suspect, your persistent efforts to force your company upon me are prompted by the fond hope of ultimately inducing me to buy a foolproof watch, a bullet-proof vest, or some other useless commodity, I may as well tell you right away that you are wasting your time. And what is more important, you are wasting mine. I require nothing to-day, and if I did I shouldn't buy it from you. I trust I have now made myself quite clear. Thank you. Good morning.'

Broglace threw back his head and laughed heartily, while Biggles watched him stonily.

'For sheer crust, your hide would make elephant-skin look like tissue paper,' went on Biggles, dispassionately, as the other showed no sign of moving. 'Are you going to find another table—or must I?'

Broglace suddenly leaned forward, and his manner changed abruptly. 'Listen, Brunow,' he said quietly but tersely. 'I know who you are and why you're in mufti*. I know the whole story. Now, I'm serious. The service has outed you, and there is nothing left for you but to be called up as a conscript, be sent to France, and be shot. What about earning some easy money— by working for people who *will* appreciate what you do?'

Biggles was about to make a heated denial when something in the face opposite seemed to strike a chill note of warning, of danger, of something deeper than he could understand, and the words he was about to utter remained unsaid. Instead, he looked at the man for a moment or two in silence, and what he saw only strengthened his suspicions that something serious, even sinister, lay behind the man's uninvited attentions.

There was nothing very unusual in the stranger's general appearance. Of average height and built, he might have been a prosperous City man, just over military age, possibly a war profiteer. His hair was fair, close cut, and began high up on a bulging forehead. His neck was thick, and his face broad and flat, but with a powerful jaw that promised considerable strength of will. But it was his eyes that held Biggles, and sent a curious prickling sensation down his spine. They were pale blue, and although partly hidden behind large tortoiseshell glasses, they held a glint, a piercing quality of perception and grim determination, that boded ill for any one who stood in his path. Biggles felt an unusual twinge of apprehension as they bored into his own and he looked away suddenly. 'I see—I see,' he said slowly.

There was a sound of laughter from the door, and a party of R.F.C. officers poured into the room, full of

---

* Civilian clothes worn by someone who usually wears a uniform.

the joy of life and good spirits; some made for the buffet and others moved towards the luncheon-tables. Biggles knew one or two of them well, and they gave him the excuse he needed, although he acted more upon intuition than definite thought.

'Look here,' he said quickly, 'I know some of these fellows; perhaps it would be as well—'

'Exactly. I agree,' replied the other, rising swiftly to his feet. 'I shall be here between tea and dinner—say about 6.30. The place will be empty then.' With a parting nod, he walked away quickly and was lost in the crowd now surging through the entrance.

Biggles sat quite still for some minutes after he had gone, turning the matter over in his mind. Then he made a quick, light meal and joined the crowd at the buffet. He exchanged greetings with Ludgate of 287 Squadron, whom he knew well, and drew him aside. 'Listen, Lud,' he said. 'I want to ask you something. Did you ever hear of a chap named Brunow?'

'Good gracious! yes; he's just been slung out of the service on his ear, and about time too. He was an awful stiff.'

'What was it about?'

'I don't know exactly, but I heard some fellows talking about it in the Alhambra last night. I believe he was hauled up on a charge of "conduct unbecoming an officer and gentleman", but I fancy there was more to it than that. Anyway, he was pushed out, and that's the main thing.'

'Did you know him personally?'

'Too true I did. I was at the same Training School with him.'

'Was he anything like me—in appearance, I mean?'

Ludgate started. 'Well, now you come to mention it,

15

he is, a bit; not so much, though, that any one knowing you would make a mistake.'

'I see. Thanks, laddie—see you later.'

'Where are you going?'

'Oh, just for a look round,' replied Biggles airily. Which was not strictly true, for he looked neither right nor left as he strode briskly along Coventry Street and down St Martin's Lane into the Strand, where he turned sharply into the Hotel Cecil, the Headquarters of the Air Board.

After the usual wait and interminable inquiries, he at length found himself outside a door, bearing a card on which was neatly printed:

AIR STAFF INTELLIGENCE

Major L. Bryndale

He tapped on the door, and in reply to the invitation to enter, walked in and found himself facing a worried-looking officer who was working at a ponderous desk littered with buff correspondence-jackets and memo-sheets.

'I'm Captain Bigglesworth of 266 Squadron, home on leave, sir,' began Biggles.

'Why are you not in uniform?'

'That is one of the things I shall have to explain, sir, but I have something else to tell you that I think you should know.' Briefly, but omitting nothing of import-ance, he described his recent encounter in the restaurant.

The Intelligence Officer looked at him long and earn-estly when he had finished, and then, with a curt, 'Take a seat, don't go away', left the room, to return a few

16

minutes later with a grey-haired officer whose red tabs bespoke a senior Staff appointment.

Biggles rose to his feet and stood at attention.

'All right, sit down,' said the Staff Officer crisply. 'Have you seen this fellow who accosted you before to-day?'

'Never, sir.'

'Describe him.'

Biggles obeyed to the best of his ability.

'You know about the Brunow affair, I suppose?' asked the other when he had finished.

'Vaguely, sir. I ascertained, subsequent to my conversation with Broglace, that he had been dismissed from service recently.'

'Quite.' The General drummed on the table with his fingers. 'Well,' he went on, 'this may lead to something or it may not, but I think we should follow it up. Your leave is cancelled with effect from to-day and you will be posted to this department for special duty forthwith. I'll see that your leave is made up later on. In the meantime, I want you to try to get inside this fellow's confidence; find out just what he is up to, and report back here tomorrow. Meet him to-night as he suggests.'

'Very good, sir.'

'And I think it would be a wise precaution if you employed the next few hours making yourself thoroughly acquainted with Brunow's history, so that you can assume his identity if necessary. Major Bryndale will give you his dossier.' Then, turning to Major Bryndale, 'I'll leave Bigglesworth with you,' he said, and left the room.

II

At ten-thirty the following morning Biggles was ush-
ered by Major Bryndale into the more spacious office
of Brigadier-General Sir Malcolm Pendersby; his face
wore a worried expression, for although he was not
exactly nervous, he was by no means pleased at the
turn events were taking.

The General glanced up as he entered. 'Well, Bigglesworth—sit down—what happened yesterday after you
left us? Did the fellow turn up?'

'He did, sir,' answered Biggles, 'and it certainly looks
as if—well—'

'Tell me precisely what happened.'

Biggles wrinkled his forehead. 'To tell the truth, sir,
it isn't easy. You see, nothing definite was said, and
no actual proposition made. It seemed to me that Broglace had something to put forward, but was being very
careful.'

'As indeed he was bound to be if he is engaged in
espionage,' put in the General dryly.

'Quite so, sir. As I was saying, it was all very indefi-
nite; his conversation consisted chiefly of hints and
suggestions, but if I may judge, the position at the
moment is this. Broglace thinks I am Brunow; he knows
Brunow has been cashiered*, and somehow or other
knows quite a lot about his history. For example, he
knew quite well what I only learnt yesterday from
Brunow's dossier—that he is of Austrian extraction and
was in the Argentine when war broke out. He knows,
too, that although his financial interests are—or were—
British, his sympathies, by reason of his parentage,
may be with Germany and the Central Powers. He is

---

* Dismissed from the Armed Forces with dishonour and disqualified
from entering public service.

working on the assumption that Brunow's disgrace has embittered him against the British—an assumption that I took care not to dispel—and that he might be induced to turn traitor.'

'But you say he made no definite offer.'

'That is quite true, sir, but it struck me that he was trying to convey his idea by suggestion rather than by actual words, in the hope that I would make the next move. He dare not risk going too far, in case he was making a mistake.'

'How did you leave matters?'

'I told him in a half-hearted sort of way that there was nothing doing, but at the same time tried to create the impression that I might be persuaded if it was made worth my while.'

'Excellent! Go on.'

'That's all, sir. Naturally, I didn't want to lose touch with him, in case you decided to arrest him, so I have made a provisional appointment—'

'Arrest!' The General opened his eyes in mock astonishment.

'Why, yes, sir,' faltered Biggles, puzzled. 'I thought that if there was a chance of him being a spy, you would arrest him on—'

'The General waved his hand. 'Good gracious, Bigglesworth,' he cried, 'we don't work like that. If the man is indeed a spy he will be far more useful to us at large than in the Tower of London*. Once we know his game we can use him to our advantage.'

'I am afraid that's rather beyond me, sir,' confessed Biggles, 'but I've done what I could, and that is the

---

* During the First World War, the Tower of London was used to house spies, prior to their trial. Some were later executed at the Tower.

end of it as far as I am concerned. May I now continue my leave?'

'Not so fast—not so fast,' replied the General quickly. 'Who said you had finished? This may be only the beginning. Pure chance seems to have placed a card in our hands that we may not be able to use without you, and I should like to give the matter a little consideration before reaching a final decision. Help yourself to cigarettes; I shan't keep you long.' He gathered up some papers on which he had been making notes and left the room.

Nearly an hour elapsed, however, before he returned, a period that left Biggles plenty of time to ruminate on the position—an unlucky one from his point of view—in which he found himself.

The General's face was grave when he returned and sat down at his desk, and he eyed Biggles speculatively. 'Now, Bigglesworth,' he commenced, 'I am going to have a very serious talk with you, and I want you to listen carefully. While I have been away I have examined the situation from every possible angle. I believe that Broglace's next move will be to make a definite offer to you, provided you do not give him cause for alarm. If our assumption is correct, he will suggest tentatively that you work for him, which means, of course, for Germany; I would like you to accept that offer.'

'Accept it?' cried Biggles incredulously.

The General nodded slowly. 'In that way we could take full advantage of an opportunity that seldom presents itself.'

Biggles thought swiftly. 'What you mean, sir, is that you would like me to become a German spy, working for the British,' he said bluntly.

The General looked rather uncomfortable. 'Without

mincing matters, that is precisely what I do mean,' he said gravely. 'Obviously, I cannot detail you for such work, but it is hardly necessary for me to remind you that it is the duty of every Englishman to do his best for his side whatever sacrifice it may involve. That is why I am asking you to volunteer for what may prove a very difficult and dangerous task. I have looked up your record, and you appear to be unusually well qualified for it, otherwise I would not contemplate the project seriously for one moment. Major Raymond, the Intelligence Officer attached to your Wing in France, speaks highly of your ability in this particular class of work; you have helped him on more than one occasion. Frankly, to handle an affair of this sort with any hope of success would be beyond the ability of the average officer. Still, the final decision must be left to you, and I should fail both in my duty and in fairness to you if I tried to minimize the risks. One blunder, one slip, one moment's carelessness—but there, I think you appreciate that, so there is no need for me to dwell on it. Well, how do you feel about it?'

Biggles thought for a moment or two. 'To pretend that I view the thing with favour would be sheer hypocrisy,' he said rather bitterly, 'but as you have been good enough to point out my obvious path of duty, I cannot very well refuse, sir.'

The General flushed slightly. 'I quite understand how you feel,' he said in a kindly tone, 'but I knew you would not refuse. Now let us examine the contingencies that are likely to arise, so that we shall know how to act when they do . . .'

Chapter 2
Algy gets a Shock

I

Lieutenant Algernon Lacy, of 266 Squadron, stationed at Maranique, in France, acting flight-commander in the absence of Biggles, his friend and flying partner, landed his Sopwith Camel* more carefully than usual, and taxied slowly towards the sheds, keeping a watchful eye on a shattered centre section strut as he did so. On reaching the tarmac he switched off his engine, climbed stiffly to the ground, and walked towards the Squadron Office to make out his combat report. He was feeling particularly pleased with himself, for he had just scored his third victory since Biggles had departed on leave.

He pushed open the door of the flimsy weatherboard building, but seeing Major Mullen, his C.O.** in earnest conversation with 'Wat' Tyler, the Recording Officer, would have withdrawn had not the C.O. called him back.

'All right, Lacey, come in,' he said. 'I was waiting to have a word with you, although I am afraid it is bad news.'

Algy paused in the act of pulling off his gauntlets and looked at the Major with a puzzled frown. 'Bad news?' he repeated, and then, as a ghastly thought

---

* A single seat biplane fighter with twin machine-guns synchronised to fire through the propeller. See cover illustration.
** Commanding Officer

struck him, 'Don't tell me Biggles has crashed,' he added quickly.

'Oh, no; nothing like that. You've been posted away.'

'Posted!'

'To Headquarters Middle East—in Cairo.'

Algy stared uncomprehendingly. 'Posted to Middle East,' he repeated again, foolishly. 'But what have I done?'

'Nothing, as far as I am aware. I can only tell you that this posting has not come from Wing Headquarters, or even General Headquarters in France. It has come direct from the Air Board.'

'But why?'

'I am sorry, Lacey, particularly as I hate losing a good officer, but it is time you knew that the Air Board is not in the habit of explaining or making excuses for its actions. You are posted with effect from to-day, and you are to catch the 7.10 train to Paris to-night. You will have to take a taxi across Paris in order to catch the 11.10 from the Gare de Lyon to Marseilles, where you will report to the Embarkation Officer at Quay 17. Your movement Order is ready. That's all. I'll see you again before you go.'

Algy sat down suddenly, and, as a man in a dream, watched the C.O. leave the office. Then, as the grim truth slowly penetrated his stunned brain, he turned to Wat in a cold fury. 'So that's all the thanks—' he began, but the Recording Officer cut him short.

'It's no use storming,' he said crisply.

'Wait till Biggles gets back; he'll have something to say about it.'

'Biggles isn't coming back.'

Algy blinked. 'Not coming back! Suffering rattlesnakes! What's happened? Has the Air Board gone balmy?'

'Possibly. I can only tell you that Biggles is posted to H.E.'

'Home Establishment,' sneered Algy. 'My gosh! that proves it. Fancy posting a man like Biggles to H.E. He'll set 'em alight, I'll warrant, and serve them right, too. Does the Air Board imagine that fighters like Biggles grow on gooseberry bushes? Well,' he rose despondently and turned towards the door, 'that's the end of this blinking war as far as I am concerned. I've no further interest.'

Wat eyed him sympathetically. 'It's no use going on like that, laddie,' he said quietly. 'That sort of talk won't get you anywhere. You do your job and put up a good show, and maybe you'll be able to wangle a posting back to 266. We shall miss you, and Biggles— I need hardly tell you that. Oh! by the way, I'll tell you something else, although you're not supposed to know.'

'Go ahead; you can't shock me any more.'

'You'll have a travelling companion, some one you know.'

'Who is it?'

'Major Raymond of Wing Headquarters. He's also been posted to Headquarters Middle East.'

'Good! I shall be able to tell him what I think of the Air Board.'

'And finish under close arrest. Don't be a fool, Algy. We're at war, and no doubt the Air Board knows what it's doing.'

'Maybe you're right,' agreed Algy sarcastically, as he picked up his gauntlets and left the office.

Ten days later, tired and travel-stained, he stepped out of a service tender at Kantara, Palestine, the aerodrome to which he had been sent on arrival in Egypt. No explanation for this further move had been asked or given; he had accepted his instructions moodily, and without interest. Kantara, Almaza, Heliopolis, Ismailia, Khartoum, or Aden, it was all the same as far as he was concerned—at least, so he had told Major Raymond when they had parted company outside Middle East Headquarters in Cairo. Where Raymond had gone Algy did not know, for he had not seen him since.

'Take my kit to the Mess Secretary's office until I fix up my quarters,' he told the driver, and then swung round on his heel as he heard his name called. Major Raymond, in khaki drill uniform, was walking briskly towards him.

'Hello, Lacey,' he cried cheerily, 'so we meet again.'

'Hello, sir,' replied Algy in surprise. 'I didn't know you were coming to Palestine, too. I'm feeling very homesick, so it's a treat to see some one I know. Why couldn't they have sent us along together, I wonder?'

'Never wonder at anything in the service, Lacey,' smiled the Major. 'Remember that there's usually a method in its madness. I had to attend an important conference after I left you in Cairo, but I got here first because I flew up—or rather, was flown up. Are you very tired?'

'Not particularly, sir. Why?'

'Because I want a word with you in private. I also want you to meet somebody; it is rather urgent, so I would like to get it over right away.'

'Good enough, sir,' returned Algy shortly.

The Major led the way to a large square tent that stood a little apart from the rest. 'This is my headquarters,' he explained, with a curious expression on his face, as he swung aside the canvas flap that served as a door.

The tent was furnished as an office, with a large desk, telephone, and filing cabinets, but Algy noticed none of these things. He was staring at a man dressed in flying overalls who rose from a long cane chair and walked quickly towards him, laughing at his thunderstruck expression.

'I don't think an introduction is necessary,' observed Major Raymond, with a chuckle.

Algy's jaw had sagged foolishly and his lips moved as if he was trying to speak, but no words came. 'Biggles,' he managed to blurt out at last. 'Why the— what the dickens—oh, Great Scott, this has got me beaten to a frazzle.'

'Let's sit down; it's too hot to stand,' suggested the Major. 'And now let us try to work out what has happened, and why we are here,' he went on, when they were all comfortably settled. 'I'm by no means clear about it, so the sooner we all know the real position the better. You probably know more than anybody, Bigglesworth, so you had better do the talking.'

Biggles smiled rather wanly as he leaned back in his chair and unfastened his overalls, exposing the R.F.C. tunic he wore underneath. 'If you'll listen I'll tell you all I know,' he said quietly.

Briefly, he told them of his encounter with Broglace, and his subsequent conferences at the Air Board. 'You see,' he explained, 'I realized that the General was quite right when he said that it was up to every one to do his best. I hated and loathed the idea, but what could I do? In the end I told him that I would go on with the business on the understanding that no one knew except himself and two persons I should name, the idea being that those two persons should act as liaison officers with me. I have only one life to lose, and I want to hang on to it as long as I can, so I didn't feel inclined to make my reports through strangers, even though they were officers of the British Intelligence Service. Sooner or later a counter-spy would get hold of the tale, and then the balloon would go up as far as I was concerned.

'Mind you, the question of going to Egypt or Palestine hadn't been raised then; that came later. Anyway, I agreed to go on with the thing if I could work with two people I knew I could trust absolutely. The General agreed, and when I named you he was quite pleased, because, as he said, apart from the question of trust, you, Algy, would be valuable because you could fly, and you, sir, because you were already on the Intelligence Staff. Now you know why you were posted.

'The next move came when I saw Broglace that evening. When he realized that I was ready to talk business he put his cards on the table and made me an offer of high wages if I would join the German Secret Service, and that showed me just where I stood. I said I'd think it over, went back to the General, and asked him what I was to do about it. He told me to accept, but if possible get to this part of the world, where the war was going to pieces as far as we were concerned, because the place was rotten with German spies—due chiefly to the activities of a Hun named El Shereef. Our people only know him by his Arab name; they very badly want to get a slant on him, and that was to be my job. They suggested that when I got here—if I did—I should get in touch with our leading Intelligence

Agent, Major Sterne. He's a free-lance, and as far as I can make out tears about the desert on a camel, or on horseback, pulling the wires through Arab chiefs and tribesmen. El Shereef and Sterne are the two big noises out here, apparently, and each has been trying to get at the other's throat for months.

'I said I'd try to get out here but would prefer to play a lone hand; I didn't like the idea of working under anybody, not even Major Sterne, although they say he's brilliant. Well, to make a long story short, I saw Broglace and told him I was prepared to fall in line with him. He wanted me to go to Belgium, but I shot him a line about being well known, and sooner or later was bound to bump into somebody who knew me. He quite saw the wisdom of my protest, and asked me to which other theatre of war I would prefer to go. I told him Palestine, and that was that.'

'But how on earth did you get out here?' asked Algy curiously.

'Ah, that would make a story in itself,' replied Biggles mysteriously. 'Broglace gave me a ring, a signet ring with a hinged flap that covered a peculiar device, and told me it would work like an oracle. And he was right. It did. I'd flown home on leave, as you know, so I went and got my machine, and instead of flying to France, went straight to Brussels. Broglace thought I'd stolen it—but that's by the way. It was a sticky trip, believe me, with Huns trying to shoot me down all the way, but I got there. As soon as I landed I was taken prisoner, but I flashed my ring and it acted like a charm. You should have seen the Huns bowing and scraping round me. I was pushed into a train for Berlin, where I had to go through a very dickens of a cross-examination from a kind of tribunal. It put the wind up me properly, and I don't mind admitting it. Then I was sent on to Jerusalem, where I reported to the Intelligence people, who posted me to Zabala under Count von Faubourg, who is O.C.* of the German Secret Service on this particular sector of the front.

'I got there two days ago, and was sent out on a reconnaisance this morning to get my general bearings.'

'But how on earth did you manage to land on our side of the lines in a Hun machine?' asked Algy in amazement.

'I didn't say anything about a Hun machine. I'm flying a British machine, a Bristol Fighter**. The Huns have two of our machines, a two-seater—the Bristol—and a Sopwith 'Pup'. They must have forced-landed over the wrong side of the lines at some time or other, and been repaired. Anyway, I slipped over right away to try to get in touch with you in order that we could make some sort of plan, and fix a rendezvous where we could meet when I have anything to report. I fancy the Boche*** idea is that I shall land over here and take back any information I pick up. That's why I'm still wearing a British uniform, although I have a German one as well.

'I daren't stay very long, or they may wonder what I'm up to. While I've been waiting I've jotted down some suggestions on a sheet of paper; I'd like you both to read them, memorize them, and then destroy it. Algy, I imagine you will be exempt from ordinary duty; the Major will be able to arrange all that. As a temporary measure I have decided on the oasis of Abba Sud as an emergency meeting-place. It's well out in the

* Officer Commanding.
** Two seated biplane fighter with remarkable manoeuvrability, in service 1917 onward. It had one fixed Vickers gun for the pilot and one or two mobile Lewis guns for the observer/gunner.
*** A derogatory slang term for the Germans.

desert, a good way from either British or German forces, so it should be safe. Here it is.'

He crossed over to a large wall-map that hung on the side of the tent, and laid his finger on a small circle that bore the name Abba Sud. 'I want you to hang round there as often as you can, and watch for me,' he went on. 'I may be flying a British machine, or a German, and in either case I will try to fire a red Very* light to let you know it's me. Then we'll land, talk things over, and you can report to Major Raymond. Now I must go. We're in touch, and that's a load off my mind. We shall have to settle details later to suit any conditions that may arise; it's all been such a rush that I haven't been able to sort the thing out properly yet.'

He rose to his feet, fastened his overalls, and held out his hand. 'Good-bye for the present, sir. Cheerio, Algy.'

Algy sprang up in a mild panic. 'But you're not going back—to land behind the Hun Lines?' he cried aghast.

'Of course I am.'

Algy turned a trifle pale and shook his head. 'For God's sake be careful,' he whispered tersely. 'They'll shoot you like a dog if they spot what you're doing.'

'I know it,' returned Biggles calmly, 'so the thing is not to get caught. You keep your end up and it will pan out all right. Remember one thing above everything. Trust nobody. The spy system on this front is the best in the world, and if one whisper gets out about me, even in the Officers' Mess here, I'm sunk. Cheerio!' With a final wave of his hand he left them.

As he walked swiftly towards the aerodrome where

* A coloured flare fired as a signal from a special short-barrelled pistol.

he had left his machine he paused in his stride to admire a beautifully mounted Arab who swept past him, galloping towards the camp. The Arab did not even glance in his direction, and Biggles thought he had never seen a finer example of wild humanity.

'Who's that?' he asked a flight-sergeant, who was going in the direction of the hangars.

The N.C.O.* glanced up. 'Looks like Major Sterne, sir, coming in from one of his raids,' he replied casually. 'He's always poppin' up when he's least expected.'

'Thanks, flight-sergeant,' replied Biggles, and looked round with renewed interest. But the horseman had disappeared.

Deep in thought, he made his way to his machine and climbed into the cockpit. The engine roared. For a hundred yards he raced like an arrow over the sand and then swept upwards into the blue sky, turning in a wide circle towards the German lines.

---

* Non-commissioned officer, e.g. a corporal or sergeant.

Chapter 3
Biggles gets a Shock

During the short journey to Zabala, which besides being the headquarters of the German Intelligence Staff was the station of two German squadrons, one of single-seater Pfalz Scouts and the other of two seater Halberstadts, he pondered on the amazing chain of circumstances that had resulted in the present situation. That the work to which he had pledged himself would not be to his liking he had been fully aware before he started, yet curiously enough he found himself playing his part far more naturally than he had imagined possible. At first, the natural apprehension which the field-grey uniforms around him inspired, combined with the dreadful feeling of loneliness that assailed him when he found himself in the midsts of his enemies, almost caused him to decide to escape at the first opportunity; but when the dangers which he sensed at every turn did not materialize the feeling rapidly wore off, confidence grew, and he resolved to pursue his task to the bitter end.

But for Hauptmann* von Stalhein he would have been almost at ease. Of all the Germans he had met during his journey across Europe, and in Zabala, none filled him with the same indefinable dread as von Stalhein, who was Count von Faubourg's chief of staff. The Count himself was simply a rather coarse old man of the military type, brutal by nature and a bully to those

* Captain.

who were not in a position to retaliate. He had achieved his rank and position more by unscrupulous cunning, and the efforts of those who served under him, than by any great mental qualifications.

The other German flying officers he had met were quite normal and had much in common with British flying officers, with the possible exception of Karl Leffens, to whom he had taken a dislike on account of his overbearing manner—a dislike that had obviously been mutual.

Erich von Stalhein was in a very different category. In appearance he was tall, slim, and good-looking in a rather foppish way, but he had been a soldier for many years, and there was a grim relentlessness about his manner that quickly told Biggles that he was a man to be feared. He had been wounded early in the war, and walked with a permanent limp with the aid of two sticks, and this physical defect added something to his sinister bearing. Unlike most of his countrymen, he was dark, with cold brooding eyes that were hard to meet and held a steel-like quality that the monocle he habitually wore could not dispel. Such was Hauptmann Erich von Stalhein, the officer to whom Biggles had reported in Zabala and who had conducted him into Count von Faubourg's office for interview.

Biggles sensed a latent hostility from the first moment that they met, and felt it throughout the interview. It was almost as if the man suspected him of being an imposter but did not dare to question the actions of those who had been responsible for his employment. Whether or not von Stalhein was aware that he, as Lieutenant Brunow, had previously served in the British R.F.C. he did not know, nor did he think it wise to inquire. Of one thing he was quite certain, however, and that was that the German would watch him like a cat watching a mouse, and pounce at the first slip he made.

Another thing he noticed was that all the Germans engaged in Intelligence work wore a signet ring like the one that had been given to him by Broglace; it appeared to be a kind of distinguishing mark or identification symbol. The Count wore one, as did von Stalhein and Leffens; he had also seen one or two other officers wearing them. His own, when opened, displayed a tiny dagger suspended over a double-headed eagle, with a small number 117 engraved below. Just how big a part it played in the German espionage system he had yet to learn.

If he had been sent to Zabala for any special reason he had not yet been informed of it. The Count, his Chief had merely said that he would be employed in the most useful capacity at the earliest opportunity, but in the meantime he was to make himself acquainted with the positions of the battle fronts. Nevertheless he suspected that his chief duty would be to land behind the British lines, for the purpose of either gathering information or verifying information that had already been acquired through other channels. In this he was not mistaken.

Of El Shereef he had seen no sign—not that he expected to. The name was almost a legend, hinted at rather than spoken in actual words. Still, there was no doubt that the man existed: General Pendersby had assured him of that. He could only keep his ears and eyes open and wait for some clue that might lead to the identification of the German super-spy.

At this period of the war the German Secret Service in Palestine was the most efficient in the world, and of its deadly thoroughness he was soon to have a graphic example. Quite unaware of this, he reached Zabala without incident, and after making a neat landing, taxied into the hangar that had been reserved for the British machines. He did not report to the office at once, but went to his quarters, where he changed into his German uniform. Naturally the British uniform was not popular, and for this reason he invariably wore overalls when he was compelled to wear it. Having changed, he made his way slowly to the Officers' Mess* with a view to finding a quiet corner in order to study a German grammar he had bought, for his weak knowledge of the language was one of the most serious difficulties with which he was faced, and for this reason he had worked hard at it since his arrival in German territory.

He had not been seated many minutes when an orderly entered and handed him a note from the Count requesting his presence at the Headquarters office immediately. With no suspicion of anything unusual in his mind, he put the book in his pocket, picked up his cap, and walked down the tarmac to the old Turkish fort that served both as his Chief's headquarters and as sleeping quarters for the senior officers, while the courtyard and stables had been converted, by means of barbed wire, into a detention barracks for prisoners of war.

He knocked at the door and entered. The Count was leaning back in his chair with the collar of his tunic unfastened, in conversation with von Stalhein, who half sat and half leaned against the side of the desk. A fine coil of blue smoke arose lazily from the cigarette he was smoking in a long amber holder, and this, with the rimless monocle in his eye, only served to accentuate his effeminate appearance; but as he took in these

---

* The place where officers eat their meals and relax together.

details with a swift glance, Biggles thought he detected a sardonic gleam in the piercing eyes and experienced a twinge of uneasiness. He felt rather than saw the mocking expression that flitted across von Stalhein's face as he stood to attention and waited for the Count to speak.

'So! Here you are, Brunow,' observed von Faubourg easily. 'You went out flying this morning—yes?' He asked the question almost casually, but there was a grim directness of purpose about the way he crouched forward over his desk.

Biggles sensed danger in the atmosphere, but not by a quiver of an eyelid did he betray it. 'I did, sir, acting under your instructions,' he admitted calmly.

'Why did you land behind the British lines?' The easiness had gone from the Count's manner; he hurled the question like a spear.

Biggles turned stone-cold; he could feel the two pairs of eyes boring into him, and knew that if he hesitated he was lost. 'Because I thought it would be a good thing to ascertain immediately if such landings could be made with impunity,' he replied coolly. 'The occasion to land in enemy country might arise at any time, and it seemed to me that a preliminary survey of the ground for possible danger was a sensible precaution.'

The Count nodded slowly. 'And is that why you visited the Headquarters tent of the British Intelligence Service?'

Biggles felt the muscles of his face grow stiff, but he played his next card with a steadiness that inwardly amazed him. His lips parted in a smile as he answered carelessly and without hesitation, 'No, sir. I had no choice in that matter. I was sent for—it was all very amusing.'

'How?'

'The idea of being invited into the very place which I imagined would be most difficult to enter. I am afraid I have not been engaged in this work long enough to lose my sense of humour.'

'So it would seem. Why were you sent for?'

'Because I had said in the Officers' Mess that I was a delivery pilot*, and he—that is, the officer who sent for me—was merely interested to know if I was going to Heliopolis as he had a personal message for some one stationed there.'

'What did you say?'

'I told him I was sorry, but I was not going near Heliopolis.'

'Anything else?'

'Nothing, sir. The matter ended there and I came back.'

'Who was the other officer with Major Raymond?'

The words reacted on Biggles's tense nerves like an electric shock; there seemed to be no limit to German knowledge of British movements. 'No wonder we are getting the worst of it,' was the thought that flashed through his mind, as he answered with all the non-chalance he could muster, 'I've no idea, sir. I saw another officer there, a young fellow, but I did not pay any particular attention to him. If I thought anything at all I imagined him to be an assistant of some sort.'

'You knew the other was Major Raymond, who has just arrived here from France?'

'I know now, sir. I was told to report to Major Raymond: that's how I knew his name. I knew nothing

---

* The pilot who delivers aeroplanes to service squadrons from the manufacturers or repair depots.

about his just having arrived until you told me a moment ago.'

'Have you ever seen him before?'

'Not to my knowledge.'

'He didn't recognize you?'

'Oh, no, sir—at least, I have no reason to suppose he did. He was quite friendly.'

The answer apparently satisfied the Count, for he looked up at von Stalhein with a look which said as plainly as words, 'There you are: I told you so. Quite a natural sequence of events.' But von Stalhein was still watching Biggles with a puzzled smile, and continued to do so until the Count told him that he might return to his quarters, although he must remain at hand in case he was needed.

Biggles drew a deep breath as he stepped out into the blazing sunshine. His knees seemed to sag suddenly, and his hands turned ice-cold although they did not tremble. 'My word! I've got to watch my step and no mistake; these people have eyes everywhere,' he reflected bitterly, and not without alarm, as he walked slowly towards his quarters.

Chapter 4
A Meeting and a Duel

He had just finished dressing the following morning
when his presence was again demanded by Count von
Faubourg. His mind ran swiftly over his actions since
the last interview, and although he could think of
nothing he had done that could be regarded as a suspicious action, it was with a feeling of trepidation that
he approached the fort. 'It's this beastly ever-present
possibility of the unknown, the unexpected, turning up,
that makes this business so confoundedly trying,' he
thought, as he knocked on the door.

As he entered the office he instinctively looked round
for von Stalhein, but to his infinite relief he was not
there. Moreover, the Count seemed to be quite affable.

'Good morning, Brunow,' he called cheerfully. 'I
have a real job for you at last.'

'Thank you, sir,' replied Biggles, with an enthusiasm
he certainly did not feel. 'I shall be glad to get down
to something definite.'

'I thought perhaps you would,' answered the Count.
'Now this is the position. We have received word that
a large body of British troops, chiefly Australian cavalry, has recently left Egypt. There is a remote chance
that they may have gone to Salonika, but we do not
think so. It is far more likely that they have been
disembarked and concealed somewhere behind this
particular front in readiness for the big push which we
know is in course of preparation. You may find it hard
to believe that twenty thousand men can be moved,

and hidden, without our being aware of their destination, but such unfortunately is the case. The British have learnt a bitter lesson, and they are acting with circumspection. I want you to try to find those troops. If they are in Palestine, then it is most likely that they are somewhere in the hills—here.'

He indicated an area on his large-scale wall-map. 'Search there first, anyway,' he continued. 'The fact that our reconnaissance machines have been driven off every time they have attempted to approach that zone suggests that our deductions are correct; if you will take one of the British machines you will not be molested. If you cannot find the camp from the air it may be necessary for you to land and make discreet inquiries.'

'Very good, sir.' Biggles saluted, returned to his quarters, put on his British uniform and his overalls, and then made his way to the hangar where the British machines were housed. He ordered the mechanics to get out the Sopwith Pup,* and then glanced along the tarmac as an aero-engine came to life farther down. A silver and blue Pfalz Scout** was taxi-ing out into position to take off, and he watched it with interest as its tail lifted and it climbed swiftly into the shimmering haze that hung over the sandy aerodrome.

'That's Leffen's machine; I wonder what job he's on,' he mused, as he climbed into his cockpit, started the engine, and waited for it to warm up. But his interest in the other machine waned quickly as he remembered the difficult work that lay before him, for the task was one of the sort he had been dreading.

---

* Single seater biplane fighter with a single machine gun synchronised to fire through the propeller. Superseded by the Sopwith Camel.
** Very successful German single-seater biplane fighter, fitted with two or three machine guns synchronised to fire through the propeller. See cover illustration.

To report the position of the Australian troops to the Germans, even if he discovered it, was obviously out of the question; yet to admit failure, or, worse still, name an incorrect position that the enemy would speedily prove to be false, was equally impossible.

'I'd better try to get word to Raymond and ask him how I am to act in cases of this sort; maybe he'll be able to suggest something,' he thought, as he pushed open the throttle and sped away in the direction of the British lines. For some time, while he was in sight of the aerodrome, he held steadily on a course that would take him over the area indicated by von Faubourg, but as the aerodrome slipped away over the horizon behind him he turned north in the direction of Abba Sud.

A few desultory bursts of German archie blossomed out in front of him, but he fired a green Very light, the 'friendly' signal that had been arranged for him by headquarters and the German anti-aircraft batteries, and they died away to trouble him no more.

He kept a watchful eye open for prowling German scouts, who would, of course, shoot him down if they failed to notice the white bar that had been painted across his top plane for identification purposes, but he saw nothing, although it was impossible to study the sky in the direction of the blazing tropical sun. 'I hope to goodness Algy is about,' he thought anxiously, twenty minutes later, as he peered through his centre section in the direction of the oasis.

He searched the sky in all directions, but not a sign of a British machine could he see, and he was about to turn away when something on the ground caught his eye. It was a Very light that curved upwards in a wide arc, and staring downward he made out an aeroplane bearing the familiar red, white, and blue marking

41

standing in the shade of the palms that formed the oasis.

'By jingo, he's down there,' he muttered in a tone of relief, as he throttled back and began to drop down towards the stationary aeroplane. A doubt crossed his mind about the suitability of the sand as a landing surface, but realizing that the R.E.8*—for as such he recognized the waiting machine—must have made a safe landing, he glided in and touched his wheels as near to the trees as possible.

Somewhat to his surprise, he saw two figures detach themselves from the shadows and walk quickly towards him, but when he identified them as Algy and Major Raymond he smiled with satisfaction and relief. 'This is better luck than I could have hoped for,' he called, as he switched off, and hurried to meet them.

'I had an idea you'd be over to-day, so I got Lacey to bring me along,' returned the Major as he shook hands. 'Well, how are things going?'

'They're not going at all, as far as I can see,' answered Biggles doubtfully. 'I'm supposed to be looking for this fellow El Shereef, but I haven't started yet, for the simple reason that I haven't the remotest idea of where to begin; I might as well start looking for a pebble in the desert. I'm scared stiff of making a boob, and that's a fact. Do you know that by the time I got back yesterday the Huns knew I had been to see you?'

'Impossible,' cried the Major aghast.

'That's what I should have said if it had been any one else, but you wouldn't have thought so if it had been you standing on the mat in front of the Count, and that swine von Stalhein,' declared Biggles, with a

---

* British two-seater biplane designed for reconnaissance and artillery observation.

42

marked lack of respect. 'I don't mind telling you that I could almost hear the tramp of the firing party when the Old Man pushed the accusation at me point blank. I went all groggy, but I lied like a trooper and got away with it. That's what I hate about this spy game: it's all lies; in fact, as far as I can see, nobody tells the truth.'

'I'm sorry, but it's part of the game, Bigglesworth,' put in the Major quickly. 'What excuse have you made for getting away this morning?'

'No excuse was necessary; I've been sent out on a job, and that's why I'm so glad to see you.' In a few words he explained his quest.

The Major looked grave. 'It's very difficult, and how the Huns knew about these reinforcements is more than I can imagine,' he observed, with a worried frown. 'No, by Jove! There is a way,' he added quickly.

'I'm glad to hear that,' murmured Biggles thankfully.

'The Australian troops are hidden in the palm-groves around Sidi Arish, but they are leaving there to-night to take their places in the support trenches. You can report their position at Sidi Arish when you get back, and it will be quite safe; von Faubourg will get a photographic machine through by hook or by crook, and he will see that you are correct. The chances are that he will launch a bomb raid to-night, after midnight, by which time the Australians will have gone. In that way we can kill two birds with one stone. You'll put your reputation up with von Faubourg, and consolidate your position, and the Huns will waste a few tons of bombs.'

'Fine! We couldn't have planned a better situation,' declared Biggles delightedly. 'And look here, Algy, while I think of it. I have been wondering how you could get a message through to me in case of emergency. There's only one way that I can think of and it's this, although it mustn't be done too often. Behind our aerodrome at Zabala there's a large olive-grove. You could fly over low at night and drop a non-committal message, cutting your engine twice in quick succession as a signal to let me know that you've done it.'

'It sounds desperate,' observed Algy doubtfully.

'It is, but it would only be done to meet desperate circumstances.'

'Quite, and I think it's a good idea,' broke in the Major. 'I've only one more thing to say. I'm afraid you won't like it, but an idea has been put up to me by H.Q., although they have no idea, of course, of the means I might employ to carry it out. As you are probably aware, the German troops along a wide sector of this front get their water by a pipe-line that is fed from the reservoir just north of your aerodrome.'

'I've noticed the reservoir from the air, but I didn't know it watered the troops. What about it, sir?'

'Can you imagine what a tremendous help it would be to us in making preparations for the next big attack if that water-supply failed?'

'I hope you are not going to ask me to empty the water out of the reservoir,' smiled Biggles.

'No, I was going to ask you to blow it up.'

The smile disappeared from Biggles' face like magic, and he staggered. 'Great goodness!' he gasped; 'you're not serious, sir?'

'Would I be likely to joke at such a juncture?'

'But you can't make troops die of thirst.'

The Major's brow darkened. 'My dear Bigglesworth,' he said firmly, 'how many times am I to remind you that we are at war? Either we go under, or Germany. The Germans wouldn't die of thirst anyway; they would merely be seriously inconvenienced.'

'But am I not taking enough risks already, without

going about blowing things up?' complained Biggles bitterly. 'It sounds a tall order to me.'

'On consideration you may find that it is not so difficult as you imagine. I can supply you with the instrument, a small but powerful bomb—in fact, I brought it with me on the off-chance. You could conceal it in your machine, and hide it when you got back; put it in a safe place until you are ready to use it. Then all you would have to do would be to touch off the time-fuse, set, say, for half an hour, and return to your quarters. That's all.'

'All! By Gosh! and enough, too,' cried Biggles. 'All right, sir,' he added quickly, in a resigned tone. 'Get me the gadget and I'll put it in my machine; I'll see what I can do.'

A small but heavy square box was quickly trans-ferred from the back seat of the R.E. 8 to the underseat pocket of the Pup, and Biggles prepared to take his departure. 'It's going to be jolly awkward if the Huns want me to collect information, as I expect they will,' he observed thoughtfully. 'I wish you could arrange for some dummy camps, or aerodromes, to be put up so that I can report—' He broke off abruptly and stared upwards.

The others, following the direction of his eyes, saw a tiny aeroplane, looking like a silver and blue hum-ming bird, flash in the sun as it turned, and then race nose down towards them.

Biggles recognized the machine instantly, and under-stood exactly what had happened. 'It's Leffens,' he yelled, 'the cunning devil's followed me. He's spotted me talking to you. Swing my prop, Algy—quick.'

He leapt into the cockpit of the Pup as the silver and blue Pfalz roared overhead, with the pilot hanging over the side staring at them.

In answer to Biggles' shrill cry of alarm Algy darted to the propeller of the Pup, and at the word 'contact', swung it with the ability of long practice. The engine was still hot, and almost before he could jump clear the machine was racing over the sand, leaving a swirling cloud of dust in its wake.

Biggles, crouching low in the cockpit, was actuated by one overwhelming impulse as he tore into the air, which was to prevent the Pfalz pilot from reaching Zabala and there denouncing him. That Leffens was flying at such an out-of-the-way spot by pure chance he did not for one moment believe; he knew instinctively that he had been followed, possibly at von Stalhein's instructions—but that was immaterial. The only thing that really mattered was that Leffens had seen him at what could only be a pre-arranged rendezvous with British R.F.C. officers, and he had no delusions about how the man would act or what the result would be. He knew that if he was to continue his work—and possibly the whole success of the British campaign in Palestine hung on his efforts—Leffens must not be allowed to return to Zabala.

Nevertheless, it looked as if he would succeed in getting back, and indeed he had every opportunity of doing so, for his flying start had given him a clear lead of at least two miles. But suddenly he did a curious thing: he turned in a wide circle and headed back towards the oasis. It may have been that he felt safe from pursuit; it may have been that he did not give Biggles credit for acting as promptly as he did; or it may have been that he wished to confirm some detail on the ground. Be that as it may, the fact remains that he turned, and had actually started a second dive towards the oasis when he saw the Pup zooming towards him like an avenging angel. He turned back

46

sharply on his original course and sought to escape, but he had left it too late, for the Pup was slightly faster than the Pfalz.

Biggles pulled up the oil pressure handle of his Constantinesco* synchronizing gear and fired a short burst to warm his guns. His lips were set in a thin straight line, and with eyes fixed on the other machine he watched the gap close between them. He had no compunction about forcing a combat with Leffens. Quite apart from the fact that the German disliked him, or possibly suspected him, and was therefore a permanent source of danger, he now knew too much. Yet he was by no means a foeman to be despised, for six victories had already been recorded against his name in the squadron game-book**.

Biggles' hand closed over his firing lever, and he sent a stream of bullets down the wake of the fleeing scout. The range was, he knew, far too long for effective shooting, but the burst had the desired effect, and his lips parted slightly in a mirthless smile as he saw the Pfalz begin to sideslip.

'He's nervous,' was his unspoken thought, as he began to climb into position for attack.

But Leffens was looking back over his shoulder and started off on an erratic course to throw his pursuer off his mark. But it availed him little; in fact, in the end such tactics proved to be a disadvantage, for the manoeuvre caused him to lose speed, and with the Pup roaring down on his tail he was compelled to turn and fight.

With the cold deliberation of long experience, Biggles

* The synchronizing gear for machine-guns which interrupts the firing mechanism ensuring that the bullets do not hit the propeller blades but pass safely between them.
** Record of all enemy aircraft shot down by squadron members.

47

waited until he saw the stabbing tongues of flame leaping from the Pfalz's Spandau guns, and then he shoved the joystick forward with both hands. Straight down across the nose of the black-crossed machine he roared like a meteor, and then pulled up in a vertical Immelmann turn*. It was a brilliant move, beautifully executed, and before Leffens could grasp just what had happened the Pup was on his tail, raking the beautifully streamlined fuselage with lead.

But the Pfalz pilot was by no means beaten. He whirled round in a lightning turn and sent a stream of tracer bullets in the direction of the Pup. Biggles felt them hitting his machine, and flinched as he remembered the bomb under his seat, but he did not turn.

The German, unable to face the hail of lead that he knew was shooting his machine to pieces about him, acted with the speed of despair and took the only course left open to him: he flung joystick and rudder-bar over and spun earthward. But if he hoped by this means to throw Biggles off his tail he was doomed to disappointment: not for nothing had his opponent fought half a hundred such combats. The spin was the obvious course, and for a pilot to take the obvious course when fighting a superior foeman is suicidal, for the other man is prepared for the move and acts accordingly.

Leffens, grasping the side of his fuselage with his left hand, and still holding the machine in a spin, looked back, and saw the Pup spinning down behind him. He knew he could not spin for ever. Sooner or later he would have to pull out or crash into the sun-baked surface of the wilderness.

* The manoeuvre consists of a half roll off the top of a loop thereby quickly reversing the direction of flight. Named after Max Immelman, successful German fighter pilot 1914–1916 with seventeen victories, who was the first to use this turn in combat.

Biggles knew it, too, and waited with the calculating patience of the experienced air fighter. He saw the earth, a whirling band of brown and yellow, floating up to meet him, and saw the first movement of the Pfalz's tail as the German pilot kicked on top rudder to pull out of the spin. With his right hand gripping the firing lever he levelled out, took the silver and blue machine in his sights, and as its nose came up, fired. The range was too close to miss. The stricken Pfalz reared high into the air like a rocketing pheasant as the pilot convulsively jerked the joystick into his stomach; it whipped over and down in a vicious engine stall, and plunged nose first into the earth. Biggles could hear the crash above the noise of his engine, and caught his breath as a cloud of dust rose high into the air.

He passed his hand over his face, feeling suddenly limp, and circled round the wreck at stalling speed. In all directions stretched the wilderness, flat, monotonous, and forbidding, broken here and there by straggling camel-thorn bushes. The thought occurred to him that the German pilot might not have been killed outright, and the idea of leaving a wounded man in the waterless desert filled him with horror.

'I shall have to go down,' he muttered savagely. 'I don't want to, but I shall have to; I can't just leave him.'

He chose an open space as near as possible to the crash, landed safely, and hurried towards the shattered remains of the German machine. One glance told him all he needed to know. Karl Leffens was stone dead, shot through the head. He was lying in the wreckage with his right hand outflung. His glove had been thrown off, and Biggles caught the gleam of yellow metal. Stepping nearer, he saw that it was the signet ring, shining in the sunlight. Automatically, he stooped and picked it up and dropped it in his pocket with a muttered, 'Might be useful—one never knows.'

Then he saluted his fallen opponent. 'Sorry, Leffens,' he said in a low voice, 'but it was either you or me for it. Your people threw the hammer into the works, so you can't blame anyone but yourself for the consequences.' Then, making a mental note to ask Algy to send out a burying party, he took off and returned to the oasis. But of the R.E.8 there was no sign, so he turned again and headed back towards Zabala.

On the way he unfolded his map and looked up the position of Sidi Arish, and smiled grimly when he saw that it was on the fringe of the area pointed out to him by von Faubourg. 'I hope the Old Man* will think I have done a good morning's work,' he murmured, as he opened his throttle wide and put his nose down for more speed.

* Slang: person in authority, the Commanding Officer.

Chapter 5
The New Bullet

It may have been fortunate for Biggles that by the time
he reached Zabala a slight wind had got up and was
sweeping low clouds of dust across the sandy expanse
that served as the aerodrome, and that its direction
made it necessary for him to swing round over the
sheds in order to land. But it was not luck that made
him look carefully below, and to left and right, as he
skimmed in over the tarmac in order to see who was
about. Thus it was that his eyes fell on von Stalhein
standing alone on the lee side of the special hangar.
There was nothing unusual about that, but with Biggles
the circumstances were definitely unusual, for on the
floor of his cockpit reposed an object that could hardly
fail to excite the German's curiosity if he saw it. It was
the explosive charge provided by Major Raymond.

It was not very large; indeed, it would have gone
into the side pocket of his tunic; but the bulge would
have been conspicuous, and it was not customary for
airmen to fly with bulging pockets while canvas slots
and cavities were provided in aeroplanes for the recep-
tion of such trifles as Very pistols, maps, and note-
books.

Consequently Biggles deliberately overshot and finished his run on the far side of the aerodrome in a
slight dip that would conceal the lower part of his
machine from watchers on the tarmac. He reached far
over the side of the cockpit and dropped the bomb
lightly on the sand with confidence, for as far as he

51

knew that part of the aerodrome was seldom visited by any one, and the small object would hardly be likely to attract attention if a pilot did happen to see it.

It was as well that he took this precaution, for von Stalhein was waiting for him outside the hangar when he taxied in. Biggles nodded casually as he switched off, and without waiting to remove his flying kit set off in the direction of Headquarters 'Just a minute; where have you been?' von Stalhein called after him.

'I have been making a reconnaissance over the Jebel-Tel country—why?' replied Biggles carelessly.

'Did you see anything of Leffens? I believe he was going somewhere in that direction.'

'I saw a blue and silver machine—those are his colours, aren't they?'

The German's eyes never left Biggles' face. 'So! you saw him?' he exclaimed.

'I've said so, haven't I?' answered Biggles shortly. 'Is there anything particularly funny about that, if he was working in the same area? The heat made visibility bad, but I think it was his machine. I wish he'd keep away from me in the air; if the British see him hanging about without him attacking they may wonder why.'

'Did you have any trouble?'

'Nothing to speak of. But I've got an important report to make, so I can't stay talking now.' So saying, Biggles turned on his heel and walked quickly in the direction of the fort.

There was an odd expression on the Count's face as he looked up from his desk and saw who his visitor was. 'Well, what is it?' he asked irritably.

'The Australian troops are hidden among the palms around Sidi Arish, sir,' stated Biggles, without preamble.

A look of astonishment spread over the Count's face,

52

but it was quickly replaced by another in which grim humour, not unmixed with suspicion, was evident. 'So!' he said, nodding his head slowly. 'So! Where is Hauptmann von Stalhein?'

'On the tarmac, sir—or he was a moment ago.'

'Ask him to come here at once. That's all.'

Biggles left the room with the feeling that something had gone wrong, although he could not imagine what it was. Had the Count been pleased with his report, or had he not? He did not know, and the more he thought about it the less was he able to decide. He hurried around the corner of the sheds in search of von Stalhein, and then stepped back quickly as he saw him. For a moment he watched, wondering what he was doing, for he appeared to be working on the Pup's engine.

Biggles heard footsteps approaching, and rather than be found in the act of spying on his superior officer, he stepped out into the open and walked towards von Stalhein, who was now examining something that he held in the palm of his hand, something that he dropped quickly into his pocket when he heard some one coming.

'Will you please report to the Count immediately,' Biggles told him with an assurance he was far from feeling.

'Certainly,' replied the other. 'I shall be glad to see him,' he added, with a suspicion of a sneer, and limped off towards the fort without another word.

Biggles watched him go with mixed feelings.

'What the dickens was he up to?' he muttered in a mystified tone, as the German disappeared through the entrance to the fort. He took a swift pace or two to where von Stalhein had been standing. One glance, and he knew what had happened, for there, plain to see in the cowling, was a small round hole that could only have been made by one thing—a bullet. His heart gave an unpleasant lurch as he realised just what it implied, and his teeth came together with a click. 'That cunning devil misses nothing,' he growled savagely. 'He knows now that I've been under fire.' Then, seized by a sudden alarm, he lifted the cowling, and looking underneath, saw what he had feared. In a direct line with the puncture in the cowling there was another jagged hole in the wooden pattern that divided the engine from the cockpit. But the hole did not go right through. The bullet must have been stopped by it, in which case it should still be sticking in the stout ash board; but it was not.

'He found it, and he's dug it out with his pen-knife,' thought Biggles, moistening his lips. 'He'll know it's a German bullet,' he went on, thinking swiftly, with his brain trying to grasp the full purport of the new peril. then he gave a sigh of relief as an avenue of escape presented itself. 'It might have been fired some time ago; if he says anything about it I can say that it's always been there—was probably one of he shots fired by the Hun who brought the machine down,' he decided, turning towards the aerodrome buildings, for he did not want von Stalhein to return and see him examining the machine.

For a moment or two he was tempted to turn and jump into the machine and escape to the British lines while he still had an opportunity of doing so, but he fought back the desire, and then started as his eyes fell on two soldiers who had appeared round the corner of the hangars. He noticed that they carried rifles. They stopped when they saw him and leaned carelessly against the side of the hangar. 'Watching me, eh? You'd have shot me too, I expect, if I'd tried to get back into that machine,' he thought banefully. 'Well, now we know where we are, so I might as well go and get some lunch; it looks as if it might be my last.'

He walked unhurriedly to his room, changed, and then strolled into the ante-room of the Mess, where a number of officers were lounging prior to going in to lunch. A word or two of conversation that was going on between a small group at the bar reached his ears, and a cold shiver ran down his spine as he deliberately paused to listen. 'Leffens . . . late . . . new bullets . . .' were some of the words he heard.

In the ordinary way most of the regular flying officers ignored him, no doubt on account of his assumed traitorous character—not that this worried him in the least—but one of them, whose name he knew to be Otto Brandt, now detached himself from the group and came towards him.

'Haff you seen Leffens?' he asked, anxiously, in fair English.

Biggles felt all eyes on him as he replied, 'Yes, I saw him this morning, or I thought I did, near Jebel-Tel, but I was not absolutely certain. Why?'

'He hass not come back. It is tragic—very bad,' replied the German heavily.

'Very bad?' queried Biggles, raising his eyebrows.

'*Ja*, very bad—if he has fell. He was making test of the new bullets that came only yesterday. If he has fell in the British trench they will know of our new bullets at once, which is very bad for us.'

'Yes,' said Biggles, vaguely, in a strangled voice, wondering how he managed to speak at all, for his heart seemed to have stopped beating. He walked over to the window and stared out across the dusty aerodrome. 'So Leffens was carrying a new type of bullet,' he breathed, 'and von Stalhein has found one of them in my machine. 'That'll take a bit of explaining. Well,

55

if they'll only give me until to-night I'll blow up their confounded reservoir, and then they can shoot me if they like.'

With these disturbing thoughts running through his head he walked through to the dining-room, had lunch, and then repaired to the aerodrome, observing that the two soldiers still followed him discreetly at a respectful distance. He was just in time to see a two-seater Halberstadt* take off and head towards the lines. Half a dozen Pfalz scouts followed it at once and took station just above and behind it.

'There goes the photographic machine with an escort,' he thought dispassionately, as they disappeared into the haze. He wondered vaguely what von Stalhein was doing, and how long it would be before he was confronted with Leffen's bullet and accused of double dealing; but then, deciding that it was no use meeting trouble half-way, he turned leisurely towards the pilot's map-room, where he studied the position of the reservoir, which was a well-known landmark. Satisfied that he could find the place in the dark, he returned to his quarters, to plan the recovery of the bomb which he had left on at the aerodrome, and await whatever might befall.

He had not long to wait, Heavy footsteps, accompanied by the unmistakable dragging stride of von Stalhein, sounded in the passage. They halted outside the door, which was thrown open. The Count and von Stalhein stood on the threshold.

'May we come in?' inquired von Stalhein, rather unnecessarily, tapping the end of his cigarette with his

---

* German two-seater fighter and ground attack biplane with two machine guns, one synchronised to fire through the propeller for the pilots use.

forefinger to knock off the ash, a curious habit that Biggles had often noticed.

'Of course,' he replied quickly. 'There isn't much room, but—'

'That's all right,' went on von Stalhein easily. 'The Chief would like to ask you a question or two.'

'I will do my best to answer it, you may be sure,' replied Biggles. Through the window, out of the corner of his eye, he saw the Halberstadt and its escort glide in, but his interest in them was short-lived, for the Count was speaking.

'Brunow, this morning you reported to me that you had located a division of Australian cavalry at Sidi Arish.' It was both a statement and a question.

'I did, sir.'

'Why?'

Biggles was genuinely astonished. 'I'm afraid I don't quite understand what you mean,' he answered frankly, with a puzzled look from one to the other.

'Then I will make the position clear,' went on the Count, evenly. 'The story I told you of the movement of Australian troops from Egypt was purely imaginary. I merely wished to test your—er—zeal, to find out how you would act in such circumstances. Now! What was your object in rendering a report which you knew quite well was incorrect?'

'Do you doubt my word, sir?' cried Biggles indignantly. 'I don't understand why you should consider such a course necessary. May I respectfully request, sir, that if you doubt my veracity you might post me to another command where my services would be more welcome than they are here?' He glared at von Stalhein in a manner that left no doubt as to whom he held responsible for the suspicion with which he was regarded.

The Count was obviously taken aback by the outburst. 'Do you still persist, then, that your report is authentic? Surely it would be a remarkable coincidence—'

There was a sharp tap on the door, and Mayer, the Staffel leader of the Halberstadt squadron, entered quickly. 'I'm sorry to interrupt you, sir,' he said briskly, 'but I was told you were here, and I thought you'd better see this without loss of time.' He handed the Count a photograph, still dripping from its fixing bath.

The Count held it on his open hand, and von Stalhein looked down at it over his shoulder.

'*Himmel*!*' Von Faubourg's mouth opened in comical surprise, while von Stalhein threw a most extraordinary look in Biggles' direction.

'Brunow, see here,' cried the Count. 'But of course, you have seen it before, in reality.'

Biggles moved nearer and looked down at the photograph. It was one of the vertical type, and showed a cluster of white, flat-topped houses upon which several tracks converged. At intervals around the houses were three small lakes, or water-holes, beyond which were extensive groves of palm-trees. But it was not these things that held the attention of those who now studied the picture with practised eyes. Between the palms were long rows of horse-lines and clusters of tiny figures, foreshortened to ant-like dimensions, that could only be men.

The Count sprang to his feet. 'Splendid, Brunow,' he exclaimed, 'and you, too, have done well, Mayer. Come on, von Stalhein, we must attend to this.'

'But—' began von Stalhein, but the Count cut him short.

* Heavens!

58

'Come along, man,' he snapped. 'We've no time for anything else now.' With a parting nod to Biggles, he left the room, followed by the others. At the door von Stalhein turned, and leaning upon his sticks, threw another look at Biggles that might have meant anything. For a moment Biggles thought he was going to say something, but he did not, and as the footsteps retreated down the passage Biggles sank back in his chair and shook his head slowly.

'This business gives me the heebie-jeebies,' he muttered weakly; 'there's too much head-work in it for me. Well, the sooner I blow up the water-works the better, before my nerve peters out.'

Chapter 6
More Shocks

He remained in his quarters until the sun sank in a blaze of crimson and gold, and the soft purple twilight of the desert enfolded the aerodrome in its mysterious embrace. Quietly and without haste he donned his German uniform and surveyed himself quizzically for a moment in the mirror, well aware that he was about to attempt a deed that might easily involve him in the general destruction; then he crossed to the open window and looked out.

All was quiet. A faint subdued murmur came from the direction of the twinkling lights that marked the position of the village of Zabala; nearer at hand a gramophone was playing a popular waltz tune. There were no other sounds. He went across to the door and opened it, but not a soul was in sight. Wondering if the guard that had been set over him had been withdrawn, he closed the door quietly and returned to the window. For some minutes he stood still, watching the light fade to darkness, and then, feeling that the hush was getting on his nerves, he threw a leg across the window-sill and dropped silently on to the sand.

His first move he knew must be to retrieve the bomb before the moon rose; fortunately it would only be a slim crescent, but even so it would flood the aerodrome with a radiance that would make a person walking on it plainly visible to any one who happened to be looking in that direction. The light of the stars would be, he hoped, sufficient to enable him to find the small box that contained the explosive.

Resolutely, but without undue haste, he reached the tarmac and sauntered to its extremity to make sure no one was watching him before turning off at right angles into the darkness of the open aerodrome. He increased his pace now, although once he stopped to look back and listen; but only a few normal sounds reached him from the sparse lights of the aerodrome buildings, and he set about his search in earnest.

In spite of the fact that he had marked the place down very carefully, it took him a quarter of an hour to find the bomb, and he had just picked it up when a slight sound reached him that set his heart racing and caused him to spread-eagle himself flat on the sandy earth. It was the faint chink of one pebble striking against another.

That pebbles, even in the desert, do not strike against each other without some agency, human or animal, he was well aware, and as far as he knew there were no animals on the aerodrome. So, hardly daring to breathe, he lay as still as death, and waited. Presently the sound came again, nearer this time and then the soft pad of footsteps. He looked round desperately for a hiding-place. A few yards away there was a small wind-scorched camel-thorn bush, one of several that still waged a losing battle for existence on the far side of the aerodrome. As cover it was poor enough and in daylight it would have been useless, but in the dim starlight it was better than nothing, and he slithered towards it like a serpent. As he settled himself behind it facing the direction of the approaching footsteps, a figure loomed up in the darkness on the lip of the depression in which he lay. It was little more than a silhouette, but as such it stood out clearly, and he breathed a sigh of relief when he saw that it was an Arab in flowing burnous and turban. But what was an Arab doing on the aerodrome, which had been placed out of bounds for them? The man, whoever he was, was obviously moving with a fixed purpose, for he strode along with a swinging stride; he looked to neither right nor left and soon disappeared into the darkness.

Biggles lay quite still for a good five minutes wondering at the unusual circumstance. Had it been his imagination, or had there been something familiar about that lithe figure? Had it stirred some half-forgotten chord in his memory, or were his taut nerves playing him tricks? But he could not wait to ponder over the strange occurrence indefinitely, so with the bomb in his pocket, he set off swiftly but stealthily towards the distant lights.

He had almost reached them when, with an ear splitting bellow, an aero-engine opened up on the far side of the aerodrome, almost at the very spot where he had just been; it increased quickly in volume as the machine moved towards him, obviously in the act of taking off. In something like a mild panic lest he should be knocked down, he ran the last few yards to the end of the tarmac, and glancing upwards, could just manage to make out the broad wings of an aeroplane disappearing into the starlit sky. For a second or two he watched it, not a little mystified, for it almost looked as if the Arab he had seen had taken off; but deciding that it would be better to leave the matter for further consideration in more comfortable surroundings, he looked about him. No one was about, so holding the bomb close to his side, he hurried back to his quarters. 'I'd better see how this thing works before tinkering about with it in the dark, otherwise I shall go up instead of the waterworks,' he thought grimly.

He reached his room without incident, and, as far as he could ascertain, without being seen. Placing the bomb in the only easy chair the room possessed, he was brushing the sand from his uniform when a soft footfall made him turn. Count von Faubourg, in pyjamas and canvas shoes, was standing in the doorway.

Biggles' expression did not change, and he did not so much as glance in the direction of the box lying in the chair. 'Hello, sir,' he said easily. 'Can I do something for you?'

'No, thanks,' replied the Count, stepping into the room. 'I saw your light, so I thought I'd walk across to say that you did a good show this morning. I wasn't able to say much about it this afternoon because von Stalhein—well, he's a good fellow but inclined to be a bit difficult sometimes.'

'That's all right, sir, I quite understand,' smiled Biggles, picking up a cushion from one of the two upright chairs and throwing it carelessly over the box. He pushed the upright chair a little nearer to his Chief. 'Won't you sit down, sir?' he said.

'Thanks,' replied the Count. But to Biggles horror he ignored the chair he had offered and sat down heavily in the armchair. 'Hello, what the dickens is this?' he went on quickly, as he felt the lump below the cushion.

'Sorry, sir, I must have left my cigarettes there,' apologized Biggles, picking up the box and throwing it lightly on to the chest of drawers. In spite of his self-control he flinched as it struck heavily against the wood.

'What's the matter?' went on the Count, who was watching him. 'You look a bit pale.'

'I find the heat rather trying at first,' confessed Biggles. 'Can I get you a drink, sir?'

'No, thanks; I must get back to dress. But I thought

63

I'd just let you know that your work of this morning will not be forgotten; you keep on like that and I'll see that you get the credit for it.'

'Thank you very much, sir,' said Biggles respectfully, but inwardly he was thinking, 'Yes, I'll bet you will, you old liar,' knowing the man's reputation for taking all the credit he could get regardless of whom it really concerned. He was tempted to ask about the machine that had just taken off, but decided on second thoughts that perhaps it would be better not to appear inquisitive.

'Yes, I must be getting along,' repeated the Count, rising. 'By the way, I'll have one of your cigarettes.' He reached for the box.

'Try one of these, sir: they're better,' invited Biggles, whipping out his case and opening it. To his infinite relief the Count selected one, lit it, and moved towards the door.

'See you at dinner,' he said with a parting wave.

Biggles bowed and saluted in the true German fashion as his Chief departed, but as the door closed behind him he sat down limply and wiped the perspiration from his forehead. 'These shocks will be the death of me if nothing else is,' he muttered weakly, and glanced at his watch. He sprang to his feet and moved swiftly, as he saw that he had exactly one hour and ten minutes to complete his task and get back to the Mess before the gong sounded for dinner, when he would have to be present or his absence would be remarked upon.

He picked up the box, opened it, took out the metal cylinder it contained and examined it with interest. Down one side was a graduated gauge, marked in minutes, and operated by a small, milled screw. On the top was a small red plunger which carried a warning to the effect that the bomb would commence to operate from the moment it was depressed.

Not without some nervousness he screwed the gauge to its limit, which was thirty minutes, replaced the bomb in its box, and slipped it into his pocket. Then, picking up his cap and leaving the light still burning, he set off on his desperate mission.

The distance to the hill on which the reservoir was situated was not more than half a mile in a straight line, but he deliberately made a detour in order to avoid meeting any soldiers of the camp who might be returning from the village. He had become so accustomed to unexpected difficulties and dangers that he was both relieved and surprised when he reached the foot of the hill without any unforeseen occurrence; he found a narrow track that wound upwards towards the summit, and followed it with confidence until he reached the reservoir.

It was an elevated structure built up of several thicknesses of granite blocks to a height of perhaps five feet above the actual hill-top, and seemed to be about three-quarters full of water, a fact that he ascertained by the simple expedient of looking over the wall. Searching along the base, he found a place where the outside granite blocks were roughly put together, leaving a cavity wide enough to admit the bomb. The moon was just showing above the horizon, but a cloud was rapidly approaching it, so without any more ado he took the bomb from its case, forced the plunger home, and thrust it into the side of the reservoir. For a moment he hesitated, wondering as to the best means of disposing of the box; finally, he pushed it in behind the bomb, where its destruction would be assured. Then he set off down the hill just as the cloud drifted over the face of the moon.

He had taken perhaps a dozen paces when he was pulled up short by what seemed to be a barbed-wire fence; at first he could not make out what it was, but on looking closer he could just make out a stoutly built wire entanglement. An icy hand seemed to clutch his heart as he realized that it was unscalable, and that he was trapped within a few yards of a bomb which might, if there was any fault in its construction, explode at any moment.

Anxiously he looked to right and left, hoping to see the gap through which the path had led, but in the dim light and on the rocky hill-side he perceived with a shock that, having lost it, it might be difficult to find again.

The next five minutes were the longest he could ever remember. Stumbling along, he found the gap at last, as he was bound to by following the fence, but his nerves were badly shaken, and he ran down the path in a kind of horrible nightmare of fear that the bomb would explode before he reached camp.

'No more of this for me,' he panted, as, tripping over cactus and camel-thorn in his haste, he made his way by a roundabout course to the aerodrome. He struck it at the end of the tarmac, and was hurrying towards his quarters when he heard a sound that made him look upwards in amazement. It was the wind singing in the wires of a gliding aeroplane that was coming in to land.

It taxied in just as he reached the point where he had to turn to reach his room, and in spite of his haste, with the memory of the Arab still fresh in his mind, he paused to see who was flying in such strange conditions. He was half disappointed therefore when he saw Mayer climb out of the front seat of the machine, a Halberstadt, and stroll round to the tail unit to examine the rudder as if it was not working properly. There appeared to be no passenger, so without further loss of time Biggles went to his room, washed, brushed his clothes, and then went along to the dining-room. As he entered his eyes went instinctively to the clock. It was five minutes to eight. Dinner would be served in five minutes, and one minute later, if the bomb was timed accurately, the reservoir would blow up.

Several of the pilots nodded to him, from which he assumed that the success of his morning's reconnaissance had been made public property. Some were in semi-flying kit, and from snatches of conversation that he overheard he gathered that they had been detailed for a bombing raid which was to leave the ground shortly before midnight.

'Going to bomb the palm-trees at Sidi Arish,' he thought. 'Well, I—' His pleasant soliloquy ceased abruptly, and he stiffened instinctively as a sound floated in through the open windows. It was the low, musical cadence of an aero-engine rapidly approaching. Aeroplanes were common enough at Zabala, but not those carrying Rolls-Royce engines. Biggles recognized the deep, mellow drone, and knew that a British machine was coming towards the camp, probably an F.E. 2D.* So did some of the German pilots, and there was a general stampede towards the door.

'Put those lights out,' yelled von Faubourg, who appeared from nowhere, so to speak, without his tunic.

'Now we see der fun,' said Brandt, who stood at Biggles' elbow. 'Watch for der fireworks.'

Biggles started, for he, too, was expecting some fireworks—on a big scale, from the direction of the reser-

---

* Two-seater 'pusher' biplane with the engine behind the pilot and the gunner in the forward cockpit.

voir—but he did not understand Brandt's meaning. 'Fireworks?' he queried, as they stared up into the darkness.

'Der new battery on der hill is of der grandest—so! straight from der Western front, where it makes much practice. Watch der Engländer in der fireworks—ha!'

The exclamation was induced by a searchlight that suddenly stabbed in to the night sky from somewhere behind the hangars; it was followed immediately by another that flung its blinding shaft upward from a point of vantage near the top of the hill.

The pilot of the British machine, as if aware of his peril, pushed his nose down for more speed—a move that was made apparent to the listeners on the ground by the sudden increase of noise. Still visible, but with the searchlights sweeping across the sky to pick it up, it seemed to race low across the back of the fort and then zoom upwards. A hush fell on the watchers as its engine cut out, picked up, cut again, and again picked up.

Biggles felt the blood drain from his face as he recognized the signal. 'Dear goodness, it's Algy,' he thought, and itched to tell him to clear off before the searchlights found him; but he could only stand and watch helplessly.

A babel of excited voices arose from the German pilots as the nearest searchlight flashed for a fleeting instant on the machine, lost it, swept back again, found and held it. An F.E. 2D stood out in lines of white fire in the centre of the beam. The other lights swung across and intensified the picture. Instantly the air was alive with darting flecks of flame and hurtling metal from the archie battery on the hill which, with the cunning of long experience, had held its fire for this moment.

Bang—whoof . . . bang—whoof . . . bang—whoof . . .

thundered the guns as the British pilot, now fully alive to the danger, twisted and turned like a snipe to get out of the silent white arms that clung to him like the tentacles of an octopus.

A shell burst almost under the nose of the F.E., and a yell of delight rose from the Germans. 'I told you to watch der fireworks,' smiled Brandt knowingly, with a friendly nudge at Biggles, and then clutched at him wildly to prevent himself from falling as the earth rocked under their feet. It was as if the hill had turned into a raging volcano. A sheet of blinding flame leapt upwards, and a deep throated roar, like a thunderclap, almost shattered their ear-drums.

Simultaneously both searchlights went out, and a ghastly silence fell, a stillness that was only broken by the sullen plop—plop—plop of falling objects. Then a medley of sounds occurred together: yells, shrill words of command, and the rumble of falling masonry; but above these arose another noise, one that caused the Germans to stare at each other in alarm. It was the roar of rushing waters.

Biggles, who had completely forgotten his bomb in the excitement of watching the shelling of the F.E., was nearly as shaken as the others, but he was, of course, the only one who knew exactly what had happened.

Some of the officers darted off to see the damage, while others, discussing the explosion, drifted in to dinner, and Biggles, saying nothing but doing his best to hear the conversation, followed them. Some were inclined to the view that the explosion had been caused by a bomb dropped from the aeroplane, while others scouted the idea, pointing out that the machine had not flown over the hill while it had been under observation, or if it *had* flown over it before they were aware of its presence, then the delay between then and the time of the explosion was too long to be acceptable. Of von Stalhein there was no sign, and Biggles was wondering what had happened to him when the officers who had gone to the hill began to trickle back in ones or twos.

They had a simple but vivid story to tell. One wall of the reservoir had been blown clean out, and the vast weight of the pent-up water, suddenly released, had swept down the hill-side carrying all before it. It had descended on the archie battery even before the gunners were aware of it and had hurled them into the village, where houses had been swept away and stores destroyed. The earth had been torn from under the guns, which had rolled down the hill and were now buried under tons of rock, sand, and debris. The Count was on the spot with every man he could muster, trying to sort things out and collect a provisional store of water in empty petrol-cans, goat-skins, or any other receptacle he could lay hands on.

Biggles heard the story unmoved. That he had succeeded beyond his wildest hopes was apparent, and he only hoped that Algy had seen and would therefore report the incident to Major Raymond, who would in turn notify General Headquarters and enable them to take advantage of it. Thinking of Algy reminded him of the signal and what it portended, but to look for the message in the darkness was obviously out of the question. That was a matter that would have to be attended to in the morning.

He sat in the mess reading his German grammar until the noise of engines being warmed up told him that the night bombers were getting ready to start, so he went out on to the tarmac to watch the preparations.

A strange sense of unreality came over him as he watched the bustle and activity inseparable from such an event. How many times had he watched such a scene, in France, from his right and proper side of the lines. The queer feeling of loneliness came back with renewed force, and in his heart he knew that he loathed the work he was doing more than ever; he would have much preferred to be sitting in the cockpit of a bomber, waiting for the engine to warm up; in fact he would not have been unwilling to have taken his place in one of the Halberstadts, either as pilot or observer, and risk being shot down by his own people. 'It's all wrong,' he muttered morosely, as one by one the bombers took off, and the drone of the engines faded away into the distance. Lights were put out and silence fell upon the aerodrome; the only sounds came from the direction of the hill, where the work of salvage and repair was still proceeding. Feeling suddenly very sick of it all, he made his way, deep in thought, to his room, and without switching on the light threw himself upon the bed.

He suspected that he had dozed when some time later he sprang up with a start and stood tense, listening. Had he heard an aeroplane, or had he been dreaming? Yes! he could hear the whistling hum of an aeroplane gliding in distinctly now, and he crossed to the window in a swift stride, with a puzzled frown wrinkling his forehead. 'What the dickens is going on,' he muttered. 'I never heard so much flying in my life as there is in this place.' The thought occurred to him that it might be one of the bombers returning with engine trouble and he waited for it to taxi in, but when it did not come his rather vague interest increased to wonderment.

As near as he could judge, the machine must have landed somewhere over the other side of the aerodrome, near the depression in which he had dropped the bomb and from which the mysterious machine had taken off earlier in the evening. 'That's the same kite come back home, I'll warrant,' he thought with increasing curiosity, and settling his elbows on the window-sill he stared out across the silent moon-lit wilderness. But he could see nothing like an aeroplane, and he was about to turn away when a figure came into view, walking rapidly. At first it was little more than a dim shadow, but as it drew nearer he saw that it was an Arab in burnous and turban. Was it the same man . . . ?

Breathlessly he watched him approach. He wanted to dash outside in order to obtain a clearer view of him in case he disappeared, so he continued watching from the window with a kind of intense fascination while his fingers tingled with an excitement he found difficult to control. It was a weird picture. The silent moonlit desert and the Arab striding along as his forebears had done in Biblical days.

It soon became clear that he was making for the fort. Biggles watched him disappear through the entrance, and a few seconds later a light appeared in one of the end windows. He knew that there was no point in watching any longer. 'I've got to see inside that window,' he muttered, as he kicked off his shoes and stole out into the corridor.

With the stealth of an Indian, he crept along the back of the hangars until the black bulk of the old building loomed up in front of him. The light was still shining in the window, which was some six feet above ground-level, just too high for him to reach without something to stand on. He hunted round with desperate speed, afraid that the light would go out while he was thus engaged, and in his anxiety almost fell upon an old oil drum that lay half buried in the sand. He dragged it out by brute strength, and holding it under his arm, crept back to the wall of the fort, below the window from which streamed the shaft of yellow light. A cautious glance round and he stood the drum in place.

His heart was beating violently; he began to raise himself, inch by inch, to the level of the window. Slowly and with infinite care, he drew his eyes level and peeped over the ledge.

He was down again in an instant, struggling to comprehend what he had seen, almost afraid that the man within would hear the thumping of his heart, so tense had been the moment. At a large desk in the centre of the room von Stalhein was sitting in his shirt sleeves, writing. The inevitable cigarette smouldered between his lips and his monocle was in place. His sticks rested against the side of the desk.

Biggles' first reaction was of shock, followed swiftly by bitter disappointment, for it seemed that he had merely discovered von Stalhein's private office, and it was in this spirit that he picked up the drum, smoothed out the mark of its rim in the sand, and replaced it where he had found it. Then he hurried back towards his room. On reaching it he crossed to the window and looked out. The light had disappeared.

Slowly, and lost in a whirl of conflicting thoughts, he took off his uniform and prepared for bed. 'I wonder,' he said softly—'I wonder.'

What he was wondering as he sank into sleep was if a slim dandy with a game leg could change his identity to that of the brilliant, athletic, hard-riding Arab who was known mythically on both sides of the lines as El Shereef, the cleverest spy in the German Secret Service.

Chapter 7
Still More Shocks

Tired out, he was still in bed the following morning when he was startled by a peremptory knock on the door, which, without invitation, was pushed open, and the Count closely followed by von Stalhein strode into the room. If any further indication were needed that something serious was afoot, a file of soldiers with fixed bayonets who halted in the corridor supplied the deficiency.

Biggles sprang out of bed with more haste than dignity, and regarded the intruders with astonishment that was not entirely feigned.

'All right, remain standing where you are,' ordered the Count curtly. 'Where were you last night?'

'In my room, sir, where you yourself saw me,' replied Biggles instantly. 'After dinner—'

'Never mind that. Where were you between the time I left you and dinner time?'

'I stayed here for a little while after you had gone, and then as the heat was oppressive—as you will remember I complained to you—I went out and sat on the tarmac.'

'Were you with anybody?'

'No, sir, by myself.'

'In which case you have no proof that you were where you *say* you were.'

'On the contrary, I think I can prove it to you, sir.'

'How?'

'Because while I was sitting there I saw Mayer land

in a Halberstadt. You can verify that he did so. If I had not been there I could not have seen him.'

'That's no proof. Every one in the Mess knew that Mayer was flying,' put in von Stalhein harshly.

Biggles met his eyes squarely. 'I can tell you exactly how he behaved when he landed,' he said quietly. 'I couldn't learn that in the Mess.'

'Send for Mayer,' said the Count crisply.

There was silence for two or three minutes until he came.

'Can you remember exactly what was the first thing you did when you landed last night?' asked the Count tersely.

Mayer looked puzzled.

'May I prompt his memory, sir?' asked Biggles. And then, looking straight at Mayer, he went on, 'You jumped out as soon as you reached the tarmac and walked back to the empennage* of the machine. You then tried the rudder as if it was heavy on controls.'

Mayer nodded. 'That's perfectly true; I did,' he agreed.

'All right, you may go,' barked the Count, and then turning to Biggles. 'Very well, then, we'll say you were on the tarmac,' he said grimly, 'in which case you may find it hard to explain how *that* found its way to the hill-side, near the reservoir.' He tossed a small gold object on to the table.

Biggles recognized it at once; it was his signet ring. It did not fit very well, and must have fallen from his finger while he was hunting for the gap in the wire. The most amazing thing was he had not missed it. To say that he was shaken as he stared at it, gleaming

---

* General term referring to the tail unit of any aircraft—the tail plane, elevators, fin and rudders.

dully on the table, would be an understatement of fact. He was momentarily stunned by such a damning piece of evidence. For a period of time during which a man might count five he stared at it dumbfounded, inwardly horror-stricken.

In the deathly hush that had fallen on the room the match that von Stalhein struck to light his cigarette sounded like a thunderclap.

Biggles' brain, which for once seemed to have failed, like an aero engine when the spark is cut off, suddenly went on again at full revs. He dragged his eyes away from the unmistakable evidence of his guilt and looked at the Count with a strange expression on his face, aware that von Stalhein's eyes were boring into him, watching his every move.

'I think I can explain that, sir, although you may find it hard to believe.'

'Go on, we are listening.'

'Leffens must have dropped it there.'

'*Leffens!*'

'Yes, sir, he had my ring.'

'*Had your ring!*' The Count's brain was working slowly, and even von Stalhein dared not interrupt.

'Yes, sir; I lent it to him yesterday morning. I met him on the tarmac, just as he was getting into his machine. He told me he had forgotten his ring, and that it would mean bad luck to go back for it. So as he was in a hurry I lent him mine.'

'But I saw you wearing yours only yesterday evening,' snapped von Stalhein, unable to contain himself.

'Not mine, Leffen's,' answered Biggles suavely. 'He suggested I had better borrow his during his absence, and told me that it was lying on his dressing-table. I fetched it and have worn it ever since. I've been meaning to report the matter.'

76

'Then why aren't you wearing it now?'

'I always take it off to wash, prior to going to bed,' returned Biggles easily.

He took Leffens' ring from the drawer of his dressing-table where he had placed it when he returned from the flight in which he had shot down the rightful owner of the ring. He tossed the tiny circle of gold on to the table with the other.

Another ghastly silence fell in which he could distinctly hear the ticking of his wrist-watch. In spite of the tension his brain was running easily and smoothly, with a deadly precision born of dire peril, and he looked at his interrogators, whose turn it was to stare at the table, with an expression of injured dignity on his face.

Strangely enough, it was the Count who recovered himself first, and he looked back at Biggles half apologetically and half in alarm. 'But your ring was found on the hill-side,' he said in a half whisper. 'Surely you are not suggesting that Leffens had any hand in the blowing up of the reservoir?'

Biggles shrugged his shoulders. He saw von Stalhein feeling in his pocket and knew he was searching for the incriminating bullet, so he went on quickly. 'I am not suggesting anything, sir, nor can I imagine how it got there. I only know that for some reason Leffens disliked me; in fact, he tried to kill me.'

'*Tried to kill you?*' The Count literally staggered.

'Yes, sir; he dived down at me out of the sun and tried to shoot me down. It was a clever attack, and unexpected; some of his bullets actually hit the machine. He zoomed back up into the sun and disappeared, but not before I had seen who it was. There is just a chance, of course, that he mistook my machine for an authentic enemy aircraft.' Biggles could see that even von Stalhein was impressed.

77

'But why in the name of heaven didn't you report it?' cried the Count aghast.

'I most certainly should have done so, sir, had Leffens returned. After I made my report to you I went back to the tarmac to hear his explanation first. But he did not come, and assuming that he had been shot down, I decided, rightly or wrongly, to let the matter drop rather than make such an unpleasant charge in his absence. Do you mind if I smoke, sir?'

'Certainly, Brunow, smoke by all means,' answered the Count in a change of voice.

Biggles lit a cigarette. Out of the corner of his eye he saw von Stalhein drop the bullet back into his pocket and knew that he had spoken just in time. 'Have I your permission to dress now, sir?' he asked calmly. 'And I should like a few minutes' conversation with you when you have a moment to spare.'

'Certainly, certainly. But why not speak now? I shall be very busy to-day; this confounded reservoir business is the very devil.'

'Very well, sir.' Biggles swung round and his jaws set grimly. 'I have a request to make, but before doing so, would respectfully remind you that I came here under open colours, not at my own instigation or by my own wish, but at the invitation—under the orders if you like—of the German Government. But it seems that for some reason or other I have been regarded with suspicion from the moment I arrived by certain members of your staff. I therefore humbly beg your indulgence in what is to me a very unhappy position, and would ask you to post me to another station, or give me leave to go my own way.'

It was a bold stroke of bluff, and for one ghastly moment Biggles thought he had gone too far, for the

78

last thing he wanted at that juncture was to be posted away.

But the Count reacted just as he hoped he would. 'Nothing of the sort, Brunow,' he said in a fatherly tone. 'I'm sorry if there has been a misunderstanding in the past, but I think we all understand each other now.' He glanced at von Stalhein meaningly. 'You get dressed now and hurry along for your coffee,' he went on. 'As far as I know I shan't be needing you this morning, but don't go far away in case I do. Come on Erich.'

They went out and closed the door behind them.

Biggles poured himself out a glass of water with a hand that trembled slightly, for the ordeal he had just been through had left him feeling suddenly weak. Then he slumped down into a chair and buried his face in his hands. 'Gosh!' he breathed, 'that was closeish—too close for my liking.'

Chapter 8
Forced Down

'Well, I must say that was a good start for a day's work,' he went on as he pulled himself together, dressed, and walked over to the Mess for morning coffee. 'I got away with it that time, but I shan't do it every time; one more boob like that and it'll be the last.'

With these morbid thoughts, he made his way to the olive grove where, after ascertaining as far as it was possible that he was not watched, he began a systematic search for the message he knew Algy must have dropped. It took him a long time, but he found it at last caught up in the branches of one of the grey, gnarled trees that must have been old when the Crusaders were marching on Jerusalem. It was merely a small piece of khaki cloth, weighted with two cartridges, to which was attached a strip of white rag about a yard long. A thousand people might have seen it and taken it for a piece of wind-blown litter without suspecting what it contained.

After a cautious glance around he secured it, opened the khaki rag, and removed the slip of paper he guessed he would find in it; the improvised rag streamer and cartridges he dropped into a convenient hole in the tree. One glance was sufficient for him to memorize the brief message. In neat Roman capitals had been printed:

IMPORTANT NEWS. SPEAK AT RENDEZVOUS AS SOON AS
POSSIBLE.

That was all. He rolled the paper into a ball, slipped
it into his mouth, chewed it to a pulp, and then threw
it away.

'What's wrong now?' he wondered, as he made his
way back to the tarmac. 'Why didn't he write the
message down while he was about it? No, of course, he
daren't do that: it would have been too risky; and he
would have had no means of knowing if I'd got it,
anyway.'

Still turning the matter over in his mind, and trying
to think of a reasonable excuse to go for a flight, he
reached the aerodrome. There were a few mechanics
about, most of them at work on machines, but nearly
all the serviceable aeroplanes were in the air. Of the
Count there was no sign; nor could he see von Stalhein.
Thinking of von Stalhein reminded him of his nocturnal
adventure and the mysterious Arab; he had little time
to think, but he felt instinctively that he was now on
the track of something important. That von Stalhein
might be El Shereef had not previously occurred to
him, and even now he only regarded it as a remote
possibility, for the two characters were so utterly different from the physical aspect alone that the more he
thought about it the more fantastic a dual personality
appeared to be. Nevertheless, he had already decided
to watch von Stalhein, and keep an eye open after
dark for the Arab who appeared to have access to
the Headquarters' offices; but at the moment his chief
concern was to get to Abba Sud as quickly as possible.

To fly without permission after having been warned
by the Count to keep close at hand would have been
asking for trouble, so he made his way boldly to the

81

fort and asked the Count if he could do a reconnaissance, making the excuse that it was boring doing nothing. To his great relief the Count made no objection, and he hurried back to the hangars in high spirits. He half regretted that he was wearing his German uniform, for it meant taking a German machine, but in the event of a forced landing on either side of the lines a German officer in a British machine would certainly be looked at askance. So more with the idea of making himself acquainted with its controls than for any other reason, he ordered out a Halberstadt in preference to a Pfalz, and was soon in the air.

He set off on a direct course for the lines, but as soon as he was out of sight of the aerodrome he swung away to the east in the direction of the oasis. Twice he was sighted and pursued by British machines, and rather than risk being attacked by pilots whose fire, for obvious reasons, he would be unable to return, he climbed the Halberstadt nearly to its ceiling, keeping a sharp look-out all the time.

He had been flying on his new course about ten minutes, and was just congratulating himself that he was now outside the zone of air operations, when his roving eyes picked out, and instantly focused on, a tiny moving speck far to the south-east. At first glance he thought it was an eagle, for mistakes of this sort often occurred in eastern theatres of war, but when he saw that it was almost at his own height he knew that it must be an aeroplane. He edged away at once a few points to the south, in order to place himself between the sun and the other machine, and putting his nose down for more speed, rapidly overhauled the stranger. While he was still a good two miles away he saw that it was a Halberstadt like his own, and his forehead wrinkled into a puzzled frown when he perceived that it was heading out over the open desert. 'Where the dickens does that fellow think he's going?' he mused, for as far as he could remember there was nothing in that direction but wilderness for a hundred miles, when the flat desolation gave way to barren hills. There were certainly no troops or military targets to account for its presence.

'I'll keep an eye on you, my chicken,' he thought suspiciously. 'It will be interesting to see what your game is.' It struck him that it might be a pilot who had lost his way, but the direct course on which the machine was flying quickly discountenanced such a theory; a pilot who was lost would be almost certain to turn from side to side as he looked for possible landmarks.

'My word! it's hot, even up here,' he went on, with a questioning glance at the sun, which had suddenly assumed an unusual reddish hue. Later he was to recognize that significant sign, but at the time he had not been in the East long enough to learn much about the meteorological conditions. But he dismissed the phenomenon from his mind as the other machine started losing height, and throttling back to half power, he followed it, still taking care not to lose his strategical position in the sun. And then a remarkable thing occurred; it was so odd that he pushed up his goggles with a quick movement of his hand and stared round the side of the windscreen with an expression of comical amazement on his face. The machine in front had disappeared. In all his flying experience he had never seen anything like it. He had seen machines disappear into clouds, or into ground mist, but here there were no clouds; nor was there a ground mist. Wait a minute, though! He was not so sure. The earth seemed to have become curiously blurred, distorted. 'Must be heat haze,' he thought, and then clutched at a centre-section

strut as the Halberstadt reeled and reared up on its
tail. Before he could bring it to even keel it seemed to
drop right out of his hands, and he clenched his teeth
as his stomach turned over in the most terrific bump*
he had ever struck. The machine hit solid air again
with a crash that he knew must have strained every
wire and strut; it was almost like hitting water.

For a moment he was too shaken and startled to
wonder what had happened; if he thought anything at
all in the first sickening second, it was that his machine
had shed its wings, for it had fallen like a stone for
nearly two thousand feet, as his altimeter revealed; but
as the first spatter of grit struck his face and the horizon
was blotted out, he knew that he had run into a sandstorm, a gale of wind that was tearing the surface from
the desert and hurling it high into the air.

He wasted no time in idle contemplation of the
calamity. He had never before seen a sandstorm, but
he had heard them described by pilots who had been
caught in them and had been lucky enough to survive.
With the choking dust filling his nostrils and stinging
his cheeks, he forgot all about the machine he had been
following and sought only to evade the sand demon.
He shoved the throttle wide open, turned at right
angles, and with the joystick held forward by both
hands, he raced across the path of the storm. At first
the visibility grew rapidly worse as he encountered the
full force of it, and the Halberstadt was tossed about
like a dead leaf in an autumn gale, but presently the
bumps grew less severe and the ground again came
into view, mistily, as though seen through a piece of
brown, semi-opaque glass. As far as he could see

* A local disturbance of air currents causing rough or uneven flying.
Due either to clouds, wind or changes in the air temperature.

84

stretched the wind-swept desert, with the sand dunes rolling like a sea swell and a spindrift of fine grit whipping from their crests. But in one place a long narrow belt of palms rose up like an island in a stormy ocean, and towards it he steered his course. From the vicious lashing of the trees he knew that the wind must be blowing with the force of a tornado, and to land in it might be a difficult matter, but with the certain knowledge that the dust which was now blinding him would soon work its way into the engine and cut it to pieces, he decided that his only course was to get down as quickly as possible, whatever risks it involved; so he pushed his nose down at a steep angle towards the trees, aiming to touch the ground on the leeward side of them.

The landing proved to be more simple than he thought it would be; he could not see the actual surface of the ground as he flattened out on account of the thick stream of air-borne sand that raced over it like quicksilver, but he knew to a few inches where it was. He felt his wheels touch, bump, bump again, and he kicked his rudder bar to avoid a clump of trees that straggled out in the desert a little way from the main group. The landing was well judged, and there was no need to open the throttle again, for his run had carried him amongst the outlying palms of the oasis. He was out in a flash, carrying two of the sandbags with which all desert-flying machines are equipped against such an emergency. Dropping to his knees, he dragged the sand into the bags with both arms and then tied them, by the cords provided for the purpose, to the wing-skids.* He was only just in time, for even with these

* Semicircular hoops attached below the wings, towards the tips, to prevent damage to the wings when taxi-ing the aircraft.

anchors the machine began to drag as the wind increased in violence, so he fetched the two remaining sandbags, filled them, and tied them to the tail-skid.

'If you blow over now, well, you'll have to blow over; I can't do any more,' he thought, as, choking and half blinded by the stinging sand, he ran into the oasis and flung himself down in the first dip he reached. The sand still stung his face unmercifully, so he took off his tunic, wrapped it about his head, and then lay down to wait for the storm to blow itself out.

He was never sure how long he lay there. It might have been an hour; it might have been two hours; it seemed like eternity. The heat inside the jacket was suffocating, and in spite of all he could do to prevent it, the sand got inside and found its way into his nose, mouth, and ears. It was with heartfelt thankfulness that he heard the wind abating and knew that the worst of the storm was over; at the end it died away quite suddenly, so removing the coat, he sat up and looked about with interest. His first thought was for the machine, and he was relieved to find that it had suffered no damage, so he turned his attention to the immediate surroundings.

The oasis was exactly as he expected it to be; in fact oases in general were precisely as he had always imagined. Some things are not in the least like what artists and writers would lead us to expect; many are definitely disappointing; very few reach the glamorous perfection of our dreams, but the oasis of the desert is certainly one of them.

He found himself standing on a frond-littered sandy carpet from which the tall, straight columns of the date palms rose to burst in feathery fan-like foliage far overhead. Nearer to the heart of the oasis tussocks of coarse grass sprouted through the sand and gave promise of more sylvan verdure within, possibly water. 'In any case the water can't be far below the surface,' he thought as he hurried forward in the hope of being able to quench his thirst. He topped a rise and saw another one beyond. Almost unthinkingly he strode across the intervening dell and ran up the far side. As his eyes grew level with the top, he stopped, not quickly, but slowly, as if his muscles lagged behind his will to act. Then he sank down silently and wormed his way into a growth of leathery bushes that clustered around the palm-boles at that spot. For several seconds he lay quite still, while his face worked under the shock which for a moment seemed to have paralysed his brain. 'I'm dreaming. I'm seeing things. It must be a mirage,' he breathed, as he recovered somewhat and crawled to where he could see the scene beyond. But the sound of voices reached him and he knew it was no illusion.

In front of him the ground fell away for a distance of perhaps fifty yards into a saucer-like depression, in the bottom of which was obviously a well. Around the well, in attitude of alert repose, were about a score of Arabs, some sitting, some lying down, and others leaning against the parapet of the well from which they had evidently been drinking. But they were all looking one way; and they were all listening—listening to a man who stood on the far side of the well with his hands resting on the parapet, talking to them earnestly. It was Hauptmann Erich von Stalhein.

To Biggles the whole thing was so unexpected and at the same time so utterly preposterous that he could only lie and watch in a kind of fascinated wonder. And the more he watched and thought about it the more incomprehensible the whole thing became. How on earth had von Stalhein got there when only two hours before he had interrogated him in his room at Zabala, which could not be less than sixty miles away? What was he doing there, with the Arabs? Why was he addressing them so fervently?

His astonishment gave way to curiosity and then to intense interest as he watched the scene. It seemed to him that von Stalhein, from his actions, was exhorting the Arabs to do something, something they were either disinclined to do, or about which they were divided in their opinions. But after a time it became apparent that the powerful personality of the man was making itself felt, and in the end there was a general murmur of assent. Then, as if the debate was over, the party began to break up, some of the Arabs going towards a line of wiry-looking ponies that were tethered between the trees, and others, with von Stalhein, going into a small square building that stood a short distance behind the well. It was little more than a primitive hut, constructed of sun-dried mud bricks and thatched with dead palm fronds.

The Arabs who went to their horses mounted and rode away through the trees, and presently those who had gone into the building reappeared, and they, too, rode away. Silence fell, the blazing sun-drenched silence of the desert.

Biggles lay quite still, never taking his eyes off the hut for an instant, waiting for von Stalhein to reappear. An hour passed and he did not come out. Another hour ticked slowly by. The sun passed its zenith and began to fall towards the west, and still he did not come. Biggles' thirst became unbearable. 'I've got to drink or die,' he declared quietly to himself, as he rose to his feet and walked towards the well. 'If he sees me I can only tell the truth and say I was forced down by the storm, which he can't deny,' he added thoughtfully.

He reached the well, and dragging up a bucket of

the life-saving liquid, drank deeply; that which he could not drink he splashed over his smarting face and hands. 'And now, Erich, let us see how you behave when you get a shock,' he thought humorously, for the drink had refreshed him, as he walked boldly up to the door of the hut, which stood ajar. He pushed it open and entered. A glance showed him that the entire building comprised a single room, but it was not that which made him stagger back and then stand rooted to the ground with parted lips. The room was empty. At first his brain refused to accept this astounding fact, and he looked from floor to ceiling as if expecting to see them open up and deliver the missing German in the manner of a jack-in-the-box. He also looked round the walls for a door that might lead to another room, but there was none.

'Well, I've had some shocks in my time, but this beats anything I've ever run up against before,' he muttered. Beyond doubt or question von Stalhein had gone into the hut; only Arabs had come out. Where was von Stalhein? He left the hut, and hurrying to where the horse lines had been, saw a wide trail of trampled sand leading to the edge of the oasis. A long way out in the desert to the south-west a straggling line of horsemen was making its way towards the misty horizon; farther south a solitary white Bisherin racing camel, with a rider on its back, was eating distance in a long rolling stride that in time could wear down the finest horse ever bred. 'So you've changed the colour of your skin again, have you, Mr. von Stalhein?' thought Biggles, as the only possible solution of the problem flashed into his mind. 'Good; now we know where we are. I fancy I'm beginning to rumble your little game— El Shereef.'

As he turned away a wave of admiration for the

German surged through him. 'He's a clever devil and no mistake,' he thought. 'But how the dickens did he get here? He must have flown; there was no other way he could have done it in the time. That's it. He was in the machine I saw. Some one flew him over, dropped him at the oasis, and then went back. They didn't hear me arrive because of the noise of the wind and I was on the lee-side of them. The Arabs were waiting here for him, and now he has gone off on some job. I wonder if this place is a regular rendezvous.'

The word rendezvous reminded him of Algy and his belated appointment. 'He'll think I'm not coming,' he muttered as he broke into a run that carried him over the brow of the hill behind which he had left the Halberstadt. As it came into view he gave a gasp and twisted suddenly; but it was too late. A sea of scowling faces surged around him. He lashed out viciously, but it was no use. Blows rained on him and he was flung heavily to the ground, where, half choked with sand, he was held down until his hands were tied behind his back.

Cursing himself for the folly of charging up to the machine in the way he had, and for leaving his revolver in the cockpit, he sat up and surveyed his captors sullenly. There were about fifteen of them, typical Bedouins* of the desert, armed with antiquated muskets. A medley of guttural voices had broken out, but he could not get the hang of the conversation; he rather suspected from the way some of them fingered their wicked-looking knives that they were in favour of dispatching him forthwith, and were only prevented from doing so by others who pointed excitedly towards the

---

* A tent-dwelling nomadic Arab. Different groups supported both sides in the First World War.

west. Eventually these seemed to get the best of the argument, for he was pulled to his feet and invited by actions and grimaces to mount a horse, which was led forward from a row that stood near the machine. The Arabs all mounted, and without further parley set off at a gallop across the desert in a straggling bunch with Biggles in the centre.

Chapter 9
A Fight and an Escape

That ride will live in Biggles' memory for many a day. The heat, the dust, thirst, the flies that followed them in a cloud, all combined to make life almost unbearable, and as the sun began to fall more quickly towards the western horizon he prayed for the end of the journey wherever or whatever it might be.

It came at last, but not in the manner he expected; nor, indeed, in the manner the Bedouins expected. The sand had gradually given way to the hard, pebbly clay, with occasional clumps of camel-thorn, which in Palestine usually forms the surface of the wilderness proper, and low rocky hills began to appear. They were approaching the first of these when without warning a line of mounted horsemen, riding at full gallop and shooting as they came, tore round the base of the hill and swept down towards them.

Their appearance was the signal for a general panic amongst the Bedouins. Without halting, they swerved in their course and sought safety in flight; in this way one or two of the better mounted ones did eventually succeed in escaping, but the others, overhauled by their pursuers, could only turn and fight stubbornly. Their prisoner they ignored, and Biggles was left sitting alone on his horse until, stung by a ricochetting bullet, it reared up and threw him. With his hands still tied he fell heavily, and the breath was knocked out of him, so he lay where he had fallen, wondering how long it would be before one of the flying bullets found him.

He had no interest in the result of the battle, which appeared to be purely a tribal affair between locals; if his captors won, then matters would no doubt remain as they were; if the newcomers won, his fate could not be much worse, for at that moment it seemed to him that death was better than the intolerable misery of being dragged about the wilderness.

Presently the firing died away and the sound of horses' hooves made him sit up. Of his original captors none remained; those who had been compelled to fight lay dead or dying, a gruesome fact that caused him little concern. The newcomers, nearly fifty of them, were riding in, obviously in high spirits at their success.

To his astonishment they lifted him to his feet, cut his bonds, and made signals that he had nothing more to fear. They tried hard to tell him something, but he could not follow their meaning, so after a brief rest he was again invited to mount a horse and the whole party set off at a swinging gallop towards the hills. Dusk fell and they were compelled to steady the pace, but still they rode on.

Biggles was sagging in the saddle, conscious only of a deadly tiredness, when he was startled by the ringing challenge of a British sentry.

'Halt! who goes there?'

Several voices answered in what he assumed was Arabic, and there followed a general commotion, in which he was made to dismount and walk towards a barbed-wire fence which he could see dimly in the fast failing light. Behind its protective screen were a number of canvas bell tents, camouflaged in light and dark splashes of colour. Nearer at hand was a larger tent, rectangular in shape, and a number of British Tommies in khaki drill jackets, shorts, and pith helmets. A young officer, tanned to the colour of mahogany by the sun, stepped forward towards the Arabs, and another conversation ensued in which Biggles could only understand a single word, one that appeared often—*baksheesh**. Eventually the officer went back to the larger tent, and presently returned with a corporal and two men who carried rifles with fixed bayonets; in his hand was a slip of paper which he handed to the man who appeared to be the leader of the Arabs, and who, without another word, turned his horse and rode away into the night followed by the others.

Biggles was left facing the officer, with a soldier on each side of him. At a word of command they moved forward to a gate in the wire, and halted again a few yards from the large tent, in which a light was now burning.

Then Biggles saw a curious thing. A distorted shadow of a man, who was evidently standing inside the tent between the canvas and the light, leaned forward; a hand was lifted with a perfectly natural movement of the arm, and tapped the ash off the cigarette it held between its fingers. Biggles had seen the same action made in reality too many times to have any doubt as to who it was; of all the men he knew only one had that peculiar trick of tapping the ash off his cigarette with his forefinger. It was von Stalhein. As he watched the shadow dumbfounded, wondering if his tired eyes were deceiving him, it disappeared, and the officer addressed him.

'Do you speak English?' he asked curtly.

'A little—yes,' replied Biggles, in the best German accent he could muster.

'Will you give me your parole?'

'Parole?'

* Money, payment.

94

'Will you give your word that you will not attempt to escape?'

Biggles shook his head. '*Nein**,' he said harshly.

'As you wish. It would have made things easier for you if you had. Don't give me more trouble than you can help, though; I may as well tell you that I have just had to pay out good British money to save your useless hide.'

'Money?'

'Yes; those Arabs demanded fifty pounds for you or threatened to slit your throat there and then. I couldn't watch them do that even though you are a German, so I gave them a chit for fifty pounds which they will be able to cash at any British pay-office. I mention it in the hope that you will be grateful and not give me more trouble than you can help before I can get rid of you; I've quite enough as it is. What is your name?'

'Leopold Brunow.'

'I see you're a flying officer.'

Biggles nodded.

'Where is your machine?'

'It is somewhere in the desert.'

'What is the number of your squadron?'

'I regret I cannot answer that question.'

'Perhaps you're right,' observed the officer casually. 'No matter; they'll ask you plenty of questions at headquarters so I needn't bother about it now. I will make you as comfortable as I can for the night, and will send you down the lines in the morning. I need hardly warn you that if you attempt to escape you are likely to be shot. Good-night.' He turned to the N.C.O. 'All right, Corporal, take charge.'

Biggles bowed stiffly, and escorted by the two

* German: No.

Tommies, followed the corporal to a tent that stood a little apart from the others.

'There you are, Jerry.* No 'arf larks and you'll be as right as ninepence, but don't come any funny stuff—see, or else—' The corporal made a gesture more eloquent than words.

Biggles nodded and threw himself wearily on the camp bed with which the tent was furnished. He was tired out, physically and mentally, yet he could not repress a smile as he thought of his position. To be taken prisoner by his own side was an adventure not without humour, but it was likely to be a serious setback to his work if he was recognized by any one who knew him. Moreover, the delay might prove serious, both on account of his non-arrival at Abba Sud, where Algy would be waiting for him, and in the light of what he had recently discovered. To declare his true identity to the officer in charge of the outpost was out of the question—not that he would be believed if he did—yet to attempt to escape might have serious consequences, for not only would he have to run the risk of being shot, but he would have to face the perils of the wilderness.

He remembered the incident of the shadow on the tent, and it left him both perplexed and perturbed. He could not seriously entertain the thought that it had been von Stalhein, yet quite apart from his unique trick of tapping his cigarette, every other circumstance pointed to it. The German was certainly somewhere in the neighbourhood, there was no doubt about that. Still, it was one thing to be prowling about disguised as an Arab, and quite another matter to be sitting inside the headquarters tent of a British post, he reflected.

* Slang: German.

With these conflicting thoughts running through his head he dropped off into a troubled sleep, from which he was aroused by the corporal, who told him in no uncertain terms that it was time to be moving, as he would shortly have to be on his way, although he did not say where. It was still dark, but sounds outside the tent indicated that the camp was already astir and suggested that it must be nearly dawn. He had nothing to do to get ready beyond drink the tea and eat the bully beef and biscuits which the corporal had unceremoniously pushed inside, so he applied his eye to the crack of the tent flap in the hope of seeing something interesting. In this he was disappointed, however, for the only signs of life were a few Tommies and Arab levies moving about on various camp tasks. So he sat down on the bed again, racking his brain for a line of action to adopt when he found himself, as he had no doubt he shortly would be, penned behind a stout wire fence with other prisoners of war.

From the contemplation of this dismal and rather difficult problem he was aroused by the sound of horses' hooves, and hurried to the flap, but before he reached it, it was thrown back, and the youthful officer who had spoken to him the night before stood at the entrance; behind him were six mounted Arabs armed with modern service rifles; one of them was leading a spare horse.

'Can you ride, Brunow?' asked the subaltern.

'Yes.' replied Biggles sombrely.

'Then get mounted; these men are taking you down the lines, and the sooner you get there the better, because you'll find it thundering hot presently. And I must warn you again that the men have orders to shoot if you try to get away.'

Biggles was in no position to argue, so with a nod of

farewell he mounted the spare horse, and was soon trotting over the twilit wilderness in the centre of his escort.

For a few miles they held on a straight westerly course, but as the sun rose in a blaze of scarlet glory they began to veer towards the south, and then east, until they were travelling in a direction almost opposite to the one in which they had started. Biggles noted this subconsciously with an airman's instinct for watching his course, but it did not particularly surprise him. 'Perhaps there is some obstacle to be avoided,' he thought casually, but as they continued on the same course he suddenly experienced a pang of real alarm, for either his idea of locality had failed him, or else his mental picture of the position of the post was at fault, for wherever they were going, it was certainly not towards the British lines. He spoke to his guards, but either they did not understand, or else they did not wish to understand, for they paid no attention to his remarks.

The sun was well up when at last they reached a wadi* that cut down into a flat plain, where the guards dismounted and signalled to him to do the same. For a few minutes they rested, drinking a little water and eating a few dates; then one who appeared to be in charge of the party handed him a small package, and indicating that he was to remain where he was, led the others round the nearby bend in the rock wall. This struck Biggles as being very odd, but he did not dwell on it. His first thought was of escape, and had his horse been left with him he would certainly have made a dash for it; but the Arabs had taken it with them, and he knew that on foot he would be recaptured before he

_____
* The dry bed of a river.

98

had gone a hundred yards. The idea of wandering about the waterless desert without a mount, looking for a human habitation, was out of the question, so he sat back in the shade of the rock and awaited the return of his escort, who he assumed had no doubt taken his predicament into consideration before leaving him.

'Those fellows are a long time,' he thought, some time later, and moved by sheer curiosity, he walked down to the place where they had disappeared. To his infinite amazement they were nowhere in sight; nor was there, as far as he could see, a place where they could hide. He ran up the side of the wadi, and standing on the edge of the desert, looked quickly towards all points of the compass, but the only sign of life he could see was a jackal slinking among the rocks. He even called out, but there was no reply.

Wrestling with this new problem, he returned to the wadi, when it occurred to him that possibly the package that had been given to him might supply a clue, and he tore it open eagerly. He was quite right; it did. The package contained an 'iron' ration consisting of biscuits and a slab of chocolate, and a flask of water. Attached to the flask by a rubber band was a sheet of notepaper on which had been written, in block letters, three words. The message consisted of the single word, 'Wait'. It was signed, 'A Friend'.

He held up the paper to the light, and a low whistle escaped his lips as his eyes fell on the familiar 'crown' watermark. 'So I, a German officer, have a friend in a British post, eh?' he thought. 'How very interesting.'

He folded the paper carefully, put it in his pocket, and was in the act of munching the chocolate when he was not a little surprised to hear an aeroplane approaching. But his surprise became wonderment when he saw it was a Halberstadt, which was, moreover, gliding towards the plain at the head of the wadi with the obvious intention of landing. With growing curiosity he watched it approach. 'If this sort of thing goes on much longer I shan't know who's fighting who,' he muttered helplessly. 'I thought I knew something about this war, but I'm getting out of my depth,' he opined. 'I wonder who's flying it? Shouldn't be surprised if it's the Kaiser*.'

It was not the Kaiser but Mayer who touched his wheels on the hard, unsympathetic surface of the wilderness, and then taxied tail up towards the place where Biggles was standing watching him. He ran to a standstill and raised his arm in a beckoning gesture.

Biggles walked across. 'Hello, Mayer,' he said. 'Where the dickens have you come from?'

Mayer gave him a nod of greeting. 'Get in,' he said shortly, indicating the rear cockpit.

'Where are we going?' shouted Biggles above the noise of the engine, as he climbed into the seat.

'Home: where the devil do you think?' snapped Mayer as he pulled** the throttle open and sped across the desolate waste.

* The ruler of Germany.
** The controls of German aeroplanes worked in the opposite direction to the British. Thus, he pulled the throttle towards him instead of pushing it away, as would normally have been the case.

Chapter 10
Shot Down

Biggles sat in the cockpit and watched the wadi fall away behind as Mayer lifted the machine from the ground and began climbing for height. He had no flying cap or goggles, for he had been carrying them in his hand when he was attacked by the Arabs on the oasis, and had dropped them in the struggle; not that he really needed them, for the air was sultry.

So he stood up with his arms resting on the edge of the cockpit, and surveyed the landscape in the hope of picking out a landmark that he knew, at the same time turning over in his mind the strange manner of his rescue. Who was the friend in the British post? He could think of no one but von Stalhein, although he would never have guessed but for the shadow on the tent. By what means had he arranged for the Arab levies to connive at his escape? It looked as if the Arabs, while openly serving with the British forces, were actually under the leadership of the Germans. 'The more I see of this business the easier it is to perceive why the British plans have so often failed. It looks as if the whole area is rotten with the canker of espionage,' he mused. Even assuming that von Stalhein had been responsible for his escape, how could Mayer have known where he was? That he had not turned up at such a remote spot by mere chance was quite certain.

Dimly the situation began to take form. Von Stalhein, disguised as an Arab, was operating behind the British lines. That was the most outstanding and important feature, for upon it everything else rested. He may have been responsible for the sheikhs turning against the British, in spite of the brilliant and fearless efforts of Major Sterne to prevent it, although Sterne had sometimes been able to win back their allegiance with gold, rifles, and ammunition, the only commodities for which the Arabs had any respect or consideration. The Halberstadt Squadron at Zabala, while carrying out regular routine duties, was also working with von Stalhein, flying him over the lines and picking him up at pre-arranged meeting-places—not a difficult matter considering the size and nature of the country. The previous day provided a good example, when von Stalhein had been flown over to try to influence the Arabs at the oasis. Later, he must have learned that Brunow was a prisoner in British hands, and in some way had been able to arrange for him to be sent down the lines in charge of Arabs who were in his pay, in order to effect his rescue, not for personal reasons but because he would rather see Brunow behind the German lines than behind the British.

The more he thought about this hypothesis the more Biggles was convinced that he was right, and that at last he was on the track of the inside causes of the British failures in the Middle East. Thinking of the oasis reminded him that they must be passing somewhere close to it; as near as he could judge by visualizing the map, both Abba Sud and the oasis where he had seen von Stalhein must both be somewhere between ten and twenty miles to the east or south-east. He turned, and pushing his Parabellum gun* aside out of the way, looked out over the opposite side of the cockpit.

---

* A mobile gun for the rear gunner, usually mounted on a U-shaped rail to allow rapid movement with a wide arc of fire.

Far away on the horizon he could just make out a dull shadow that might have been an oasis, but he was too uncertain of his actual position to know which of the two it was, if indeed it was either of them. Perhaps Mayer had a map; if so, he would borrow it. He reached forward and tapped the German on the shoulder, and then sprang back in affright as the shrill chatter of a machine-gun split the air from somewhere near at hand. A shower of lead struck the Halberstadt like a flail. There was a shrill *whang* of metal striking against metal, and a ghastly tearing sound of splintering woodwork. The stricken machine lurched drunkenly as the engine cut out dead and a long feather of oily black smoke swirled away aft.

Instinctively Biggles grabbed his gun, and squinted through his slightly open fingers in the direction of the sun whence the attack had come. The blinding white orb seared his eyeballs, but he caught a fleeting glimpse of a grey shadow that banked round in a steep stalling turn to renew the attack. He turned to warn Mayer, and a cry of horror broke from his lips as he saw him sagging insensible in his safety belt; a trickle of blood was oozing from under the ear flaps of his leather helmet.

As in a ghastly nightmare, Biggles heard the staccato clatter of the guns again, and felt the machine shudder like a sailing ship taken aback, as the controls flapped uselessly. Its nose lurched downwards; the port wing drooped, and the next instant the machine was spinning wildly earthward.

Biggles, cold with fear, acted with the deliberation of long experience, moved with a calmness that would have seemed impossible on the ground. He knew that the machine was fitted with dual controls, but the rear joystick was not left in its socket for fear of the observer

103

being hit and falling on it in a combat, thus jamming the controls. It was kept in a canvas slot in the side of the cockpit. Swiftly he pulled it out, inserted the end in the metal junction and screwed it in. Without waiting to look out of the cockpit, he pushed the stick forward and kicked on full top rudder. The machine began to respond instantly; would it come out of the spin in time? He dropped back into his seat, and snatching a swift glance at the ground, now perilously near, knew that it was going to be touch and go. Slowly the nose of the machine came up as it came out of the spin.

With another five feet of height the Halberstadt would just have managed it; she did in fact struggle to even keel, but still lost height from the speed of her spin, as she was bound to for a few seconds. Biggles pulled the stick back and held his breath; he had no engine to help him, and the best he could hope for was some sort of pancake* landing. But luck was against him, for the ground at that point was strewn with boulders, some large and some small, and it must have been one of the large ones that caught the axle of his undercarriage. The lower part of the machine seemed to stop dead while the upper part, carried on by its momentum, tried to go forward; then several things happened at once. Biggles was flung violently against the instrument board; the propeller boss bored into the ground, hurling splinters of wood and rock in all directions; the tail swung up and over in a complete semicircle as the machine somersaulted in a final tearing, rending, splintering crash. Then silence.

Biggles, half blinded by petrol which had poured over him when the tank sheered off its bearers and

---

* Instead of the aircraft gliding down to land, it flops down from a height of a few feet, after losing flying speed.

burst asunder, fought his way out of the wreck like a madman, regardless of mere bruises and cuts. The horror of fire was on him, as it is on every airman in similar circumstances, but his first thought was for his companion. 'Mayer' he croaked, 'where are you?' There was no answer, so he tore the debris aside until he found the German, still strapped in his seat, buried under the tangled remains of the plane. Somehow—he had no clear recollection of how it was done—he got him clear of the cockpit, and dragged him through the tangle of wires and struts to a spot some distance away, clear of fire should it break out. Then he sank down and buried his face in his hands while he fought back an hysterical desire to burst into tears. He had seen stronger men than himself do it, and knew that it was simply the sudden relaxation of nerves that had been screwed up to breaking-point.

Then he rose unsteadily to his feet, wiped a smear of blood from a cut in his lip, and turned to his partner-in-misfortune, for the cause of the trouble was already a tiny speck in the far distance. So swift and perfectly timed had been the attack that he hadn't even time to identify the type of machine that had shot them down.

He took off Mayer's helmet, and a long red weal across the side of his head told its own story. As far as he could see the bullet had not actually penetrated the skull, but had struck him a glancing blow that had knocked him unconscious, and might, or might not, prove fatal. He could find no other bullet wounds, although his clothes were badly torn about and his face bruised, so he made him as comfortable as possible in the shade of the rock and then went to see if he could get a little water from the leaking radiator. It was hot and oily, but it was better than nothing, so he soaked his handkerchief and returned to Mayer. Had it been

105

possible, he would have tried to save some of the precious liquid that was fast disappearing into the thirsty ground, but he had no receptacle to catch it, so he went back to the unfortunate German and cleaned the wound as well as he could. His efforts were rewarded, for after a few minutes Mayer opened his eyes and stared about him wonderingly. Wonderment gave way to understanding as complete consciousness returned, and he smiled weakly.

'What happened?' he whispered through his bruised lips.

'An Engländer dropped on us out of the sun and hit us with his first burst,' replied Biggles. 'A bullet hit you on the side of the head and the box* spun before I could get my gun going. I managed to get her out of the spin with the spare joystick before she hit the ground, but the engine had gone, so I had to get down as well as I could—which wasn't very well, as you can see,' he added dryly. 'There are too many rocks about for nice landings; but there, we were lucky she didn't catch fire.'

Mayer tried to move, but a low groan broke from his lips.

'I should lie still for a bit if I were you,' Biggles advised him. 'You'll be better presently.'

'You'd better go on,' the German told him stolidly.

'Go on? And leave you here? No, I'll wait for you.'

'Do you know where we are?' inquired Mayer, bitterly.

'Not exactly.'

'We're fifty miles from our lines, and it's fifty miles of waterless desert, so you'd better be starting.'

'No hurry, I'll wait for you.'

---

* German slang for an aeroplane.

'It'll be no use waiting for me.'

'Why not?'

'Because I shan't be coming.'

'Who says so?'

'I do. My leg is broken.'

Biggles felt the blood drain from his face as he realized just what Mayer's grim statement meant. 'Good heavens,' he breathed.

The German smiled curiously. 'The fortune of war,' he observed calmly. 'Before you go I would like you to do something for me.'

'What is it?'

'Go and look in my cockpit and see if you can find my pistol. I shall need it.'

'No, you won't,' Biggles told him tersely, for he knew well enough what was in the other's mind.

'You wouldn't leave me here to die of thirst—and the hyenas,' protested Mayer weakly.

'Who's talking about leaving you, anyway,' growled Biggles. 'Just you lie still while I think it over.'

'If you've any sense you'll go on. There's no need for us both to die,' said Mayer, with a courage that Biggles could not help but admire.

'I'm not talking about dying, either,' he declared. 'We'll find a way out; let me think a minute.' Then he laughed. The idea of an Englishman and a German each trying to save the other's life struck him as funny.

'What's the joke?' asked Mayer suspiciously.

'No joke—but it's no use bursting into tears,' returned Biggles brightly. He walked across and examined the machine. There were still a few drops of water in the radiator, but it was poisonous-looking fluid and he watched it drip away into the sand without regret. He dug about in the wreckage until he found Mayer's map, when he sat down and plotted their position as nearly as he could judge it. As Mayer had said, they were a good fifty miles from the German lines, and farther still from the British lines, but to the south and east there were two or three oases, unnamed, from which he guessed they were very small, not less than fifteen and not more than twenty miles away. Fifteen miles! Could he do it in the heat of the day? Alone, perhaps, but with a wounded companion, definitely no. Suppose he left Mayer, and tried to find the oasis where he had seen von Stalhein; could he fly back in the Halberstadt, assuming that it was as he had left it? No, he decided, for the German would certainly have died of thirst in the meantime.

The idea of leaving Mayer to perish did not occur to him. In the desperate straits in which they found themselves, he no longer regarded him as an enemy, but as a brother pilot who must be supported while a vestige of hope remained. He regarded the crashed machine with a speculative eye, and half smiled as a possibility occurred to him. Near at hand was one of the undercarriage wheels, with the bent axle still attached; the tyre had burst, but otherwise it was undamaged. The other wheel lay some distance away in the desert where it had bounced after the crash. He retrieved it and then set to work, while Mayer watched him dispassionately.

At the end of an hour he had constructed a fairly serviceable two-wheeled trailer from the undercarriage and remains of the wing spars. He had found plenty of material to work with; in fact, more than he needed. Finally he hunted about in the wreckage for the seat cushions, smiling as he caught sight of his unshaven, blood-stained face in the pilot's reflector. He found them, threw them on the crazy vehicle, and picking up some pieces of interplane struts and canvas, approached the German.

Mayer regarded him dubiously. 'You've wasted a lot of time,' he said irritably.

'Maybe,' replied Biggles imperturbably. 'Help me as much as you can while I get this leg of yours fixed up.'

'Do what?' ejaculated Mayer. 'What are you going to do?'

'Tie your leg up in these splints, so that it won't hurt more than can be helped while I get you on the perambulator.'

'Don't be a fool—'

'If you don't lie still, I'll fetch you a crack on the other side of your skull,' snarled Biggles. 'Do you think I want to hang about here all day? Come on—that's better.'

Not without difficulty he bound up Mayer's leg in the improvised splints, and then lifted him bodily on to the trailer. He handed him a piece of fabric to use as a sunshade, and without another word set off in the direction in which he judged the oasis to be.

Fortunately the ground was flat and fairly open, but the punctured wheel dragged heavily through the patches of loose sand that became more frequent as he went on. The sun climbed to its zenith and its white bars of heat struck down with relentless force.

Nowhere could he find rest for his eyes; in all directions stretched the wilderness, colourless and without outline, a vast undulating expanse of brown and grey that merged into the shimmering horizon. The land had no definite configuration, but was an eternal monotony of sand and rock, spotted here and there with the everlasting camel-thorn. There was no wild life—or if there was he did not see it. Once he straightened his back and looked round the scene, but its overwhelming solitude made him shudder and he went on with his task doing his best to fight off the dreadful feeling of depression that was creeping over him.

The demon thirst began to torture him. Another hour passed, and another, and still he struggled on. His lips were black and dry, with a little ring of congealed dust round them. He no longer perspired, for the sun drank up every drop of moisture as soon as it appeared. Mayer was more fortunate, for he had lapsed into unconsciousness. At first Biggles had tried to keep the fabric over his face, but he soon got tired of picking it up and struggled on without it. A feeling crept over him that he had been pulling the trailer all his life; everything else that had ever happened was a dim memory; only the rocks and the sand were real.

Presently he began to mutter to himself, and eyed the sun malevolently. 'I'd give you something, you skunk, if I had my guns,' he grated through his clenched teeth. It did not occur to him to leave his companion; the fixedness of purpose that had won him fame in France kept the helpless German ever before his mind. 'Poor old Mayer,' he crooned. 'Tough luck, getting a cracked leg. Why the dickens isn't Algy here; I'll twist the young scallywag's ear for him for leaving the patrol like this.'

Mayer began to mutter in German, long meaningless sentences in which the word Rhine occurred frequently.

'When we wind up the watch on the Rhine,' cackled Biggles. 'Your watch is about wound up, old cock,' and he laughed again. He stumbled on a rock, and swinging round in a blaze of fury, kicked it viciously and uselessly. He reached the top of a fold in the ground and stared ahead with eyes that seemed to be two balls of fire searing his brain. A line of cool green palm trees stood up clearly on the skyline. 'Ha, ha, you can't catch me like that,' he chuckled. 'Mirage; I've heard about you. Thinks it can catch me. Ha, ha!'

A big bird flopped down heavily not far away and regarded him with cold beady eyes. He dropped the handle of the trailer, snatched up a stone, and hurled it with all his strength. The bird flapped a few yards further away and settled again. 'You Hun,' he croaked. 'You dirty thieving Hun. I can see you sitting there; I'll knock the bottom out of your fuselage before I've finished with you.' He picked up the handle of the trailer and struggled on.

He began to sway as he walked. Once he fell, and lay where he had fallen for a full minute before he remembered his burden, whereupon he scrambled to his feet and set off with a fresh burst of energy. He topped another rise and saw a long group of green palm fronds against the blue sky above the next dip. At first he regarded them with a sort of detached interest, but slowly it penetrated his bemused mind that they were very real, very close, and very desirable. He broke into a drunken run, still dragging the trailer, and breathing in deep wheezing gasps; the palm trees seemed to float towards him, and presently he was amongst them, patting the rough boles with his hands. The place was vaguely familiar and he seemed to know exactly where to go, so he dropped the handle of the trailer and reeled towards the centre of the oasis, croaking as he saw that he was not mistaken. In front of him was the well and the hut where, the afternoon before, he had seen von Stalhein. He had returned to his starting point. He staggered to the well, seized the hide rope in his shaking hands, dragged up the receptacle attached to it and drank as he had never drunk before. Then he refilled the makeshift bucket and ran back to where he had left Mayer. He rolled him off the trailer

111

and with difficulty got some of the water between his parched lips, at the same time dabbing his face and neck with it. He continued giving him a little water for some time, occasionally drinking deep draughts himself; but when he felt that he could do no more for the sick man, he returned to the well and buried his face and arms in the cool liquid.

He still had the remains of the chocolate ration in his pocket, so he munched a little and felt better for it. Then he walked up to the hut, but it was empty, so he returned to Mayer with the idea of making him as comfortable as possible before going to the spot where he had left the Halberstadt, to make sure it was still there and undamaged. But suddenly he felt dreadfully tired and sat down near the trailer to rest. The shade, after the heat of the sun which was now sinking fast, was pleasant, and he closed his eyes in ecstasy. His head nodded once or twice, and he slipped slowly sideways on to the cool sand, sound asleep.

Chapter 11
A Night Flight

I

He awoke, and sitting up with a start, looked around in bewilderment, for it was night, and for a moment or two he could not recall what had happened. The moon was up; it hung low over the desert like a sickle and cast a pale blue radiance over a scene of unutterable loneliness. Then, in the hard, black lattice-like shadows of the palms, he saw Mayer, and remembered everything. The German's face was ghastly in the weird light, and he thought he was dead, but dropping on his hands and knees beside him, was relieved to hear faint but regular breathing.

Then he sprang to his feet as a strange sound reached his ears, and he knew instinctively that it was the same noise that had awakened him; it reminded him of the harsh confused murmur of waves upon a pebbly beach, afar off, rising and falling on the still night air. For a little while he sat listening, trying to identify the sound, but he could not; it seemed to come from the other side of the oasis, so he made his way cautiously through the palms to a slight rise from which he could see the desert beyond. As he reached it and looked out he caught his breath sharply and sank down swiftly in the shadow of a stunted palm, staring with wide-open eyes.

He did not know what he had expected to see, but it was certainly not the sight that met his incredulous eyes. Mustering in serried ranks was an army of Arabs;

at a rough computation he made out the number to be nearly four thousand, and fresh bands were still riding in from the desert, gathering together for what could only be one of the biggest Arab raids ever organized—for he had no delusions as to their purpose. What was their objective? Were they being mustered by von Stalhein to harass the British flank, or by Major Sterne to launch a crippling blow at the German lines of communication? Those were questions he could not answer, but he hoped that by watching he might discover. He was glad that whoever was in charge had not decided to use the oasis itself as a meeting-place, or he would have been found, but a moment's consideration revealed the impracticability of such a course; a body of men of that size could only parade in the open.

For half an hour he lay and watched them, and at the end of that time they began to move off, not in any regular order, but winding like a long sinuous snake out into the desert; and he had no need to watch them for very long to guess their objective, for the direction they took would bring them within a few hours to the eastern outposts of the British army.

'If that bunch hits the right wing of our lines of communication without warning it'll go right through them like a knife through butter, and our fellows in the front-line trenches will be cut off from supplies and everything else,' he muttered anxiously. 'I shall have to let our people know somehow.' As the tail-end of the column disappeared into the mysterious blue haze of the middle distance he glanced at the moon and made a swift calculation. 'It must be somewhere about eleven o'clock—not later,' he thought. 'At an average speed of six miles an hour, and they can easily manage that, seven hours will see them ready to strike at our

114

flank at just about dawn, which is probably the time they have fixed for the attack.'

He got up and ran back swiftly to where he had left Mayer. He was still unconscious, so he hurried round the edge of the oasis to where he had left the Halberts-tadt the previous day. 'If it's gone, I'm sunk,' he mur-mured, and then uttered a low cry of delight as his eyes fell on it, standing just as he had left it. 'Now! what's my best plan of action?' he thought swiftly. 'Shall I leave Mayer here and dash down to Kantara in the hope of getting in touch with Algy? If I do, I daren't land, for if I did every officer on the station would know that a German machine had landed on the aerodrome, which would mean that the Germans would know it too. That's no use. The only thing I can do is to write a message, drop it, and then signal to Algy and Major Raymond as we arranged. That's the safest way; they would be bound to find it on the aerodrome. But what about Mayer? I can't leave him here and risk a night landing in order to pick him up afterwards; I might run short of petrol anyway, and I don't want to get stuck in the desert again. I shall have to take him with me. But I had better have a look at the machine.'

He found it exactly as he had left it, and thanked the lucky chance that ordained that not only should he have landed at what seemed to be the little-used end of the oasis, but amongst the trees, where the machine could not be seen from the desert. After removing the sandbag anchors he lifted up the tailskid and dragged the Halberstadt into the open, a task that presented no difficulty as the slope was slightly downhill. He climbed into the cockpit, turned on the petrol tap, and then returned to the front of the machine, where he turned the propeller round several times in order to suck the

115

petrol gas into the cylinders. The machine was not fitted with a self-starter, so he switched on the ignition and then returned to the propellor in order to swing it. Before he did so, however, he took a leaf from his note-book, wrote a message on it, and addressed it to Algy. This done, he took off his tunic, ripped a length of material from his shirt to form a streamer, and tying the message in it with a pebble to give it weight, put it in his pocket and returned to the engine.

In the warm air it started at once, and in the stillness of the desert night the din that it made was so appalling that he started back in alarm. 'Great Scott! what a row,' he muttered as he climbed quickly into his seat and began to taxi carefully to the place where he had left the German. Mayer was still unconscious and lying in the same position, so he set to work on the formidable task of getting him into the rear cockpit. This he finally managed to do with no small exertion by picking him up in the 'fireman's grip' and dropping him bodily over the side; the unfortunate man fell in a heap, but there was no help for it, and as Biggles observed to himself as he got him into a sitting position, in the seat, with the safety belt round his waist, 'He's unconscious, so it isn't hurting him, anyway.'

Before climbing back into his cockpit he looked long and critically down the track over which he would have to take off. 'If I hit a brick, there's going to be a nasty mess,' was his unspoken thought as he eased the throttle open and held the stick slightly forward. But any fears he may have had on the matter of buckling a wheel—with calamitous results—against a rock were set at rest as the machine rose gracefully into the air, and he settled down to his task with a sigh of relief and satisfaction.

It was a weird experience, flying over the moonlit

desert that in the early days of history had been the scene of wars of extermination, and the pictures of many famous Biblical characters floated up in his imagination. Below him, more than twenty centuries before, Joseph had wandered in his coat of many colours, and the Prodigal Son had wasted his money in riotous living. 'There wouldn't be much for him to spend his money on to-day, I'm afraid,' thought Biggles whimsically, as he surveyed the barren land that once, before the great rivers had dried up, had flowed with milk and honey. 'Still, maybe it will regain some of its prosperity again one day when human beings come to their senses and stop fighting each other,' he mused, as he turned his nose a little more to the north, in order to avoid being heard by the raiders, and von Stalhein in particular, who he suspected was leading them, and who would certainly recognize the drone of his Mercedes engine.

A white wavering finger suddenly probed the sky some distance ahead, and he knew he was approaching the British lines. Soon afterwards a blood-red streak of flame flashed across his vision, and he knew that the anti-aircraft gunners were at work. He was not very perturbed, for he had climbed fairly high and knew that the chances of being hit were very remote; but as the archie barrage grew more intense, he throttled back and began a long glide towards the aerodrome at Kantara. Several searchlight beams were combing the sky for him, but he avoided them easily and smiled grimly as the lights of the aerodrome came into view. 'If I was carrying a load of bombs instead of a sick German, those fellows would soon be getting what they are asking for,' he growled, and shut off his engine as he dived steeply towards his objective. White lines of tracer bullets were streaking upwards, but in the darkness the shooting was chiefly guesswork and none of them came near him, although he realized that this state of affairs was likely to change when he opened his engine and by so doing disclosed his whereabouts.

With one hand on the throttle and the message lying on his lap, he raced low over the aerodrome; when he reached the middle he tossed the message overboard, and opened and closed the throttle twice in quick succession. Then he pulled it wide open and zigzagged out of the vicinity, like a startled bird, as the searchlights swung round and every gun within range redoubled its efforts to hit him. But he was soon outside their field of fire and racing nose down towards the German lines. Once he glanced back to satisfy himself that Mayer was still unconscious. 'If he'd come round just now he might well have wondered what the dickens was going on,' he thought, 'and he might have asked some awkward questions when we got back—or caused the Count to ask some. As it is, he'll wonder how on earth he got home when he wakes up and finds himself in Zabala.'

The rest of the flight was simply a fight against the lassitude that overtakes all pilots after a period of flying, when they have nothing to do but fly on a straight course, for the comfortable warmth that fills the cockpit, due to the proximity of the engine, induces sleep, and the regular drone of the wind in the wires becomes a lullaby hard to resist. He found himself nodding more than once, and each time he started up and beat his hands on the side of the cockpit, and held his face outside the shield of the windscreen to allow the cool slipstream to play on his weary eyes.

The scattered lights of Zabala came into sight at last, and he glided down without waiting for landing lights to be put out. There was no wind, so he was able to land directly towards the sheds, and finished his run within a few yards of them. He switched off the engine and sat quite still, for now that his task was finished, and the need for mental and physical energy no longer required, he let himself go, and his aching nerves collapsed like a piece of taut elastic when it is cut in the middle.

As in a queer sort of dream he heard voices calling, and brisk words of command; but they seemed to be far away and barely penetrated his rapidly failing consciousness, and he paid no attention to them. He blinked owlishly as a flashlight was turned on his face, and felt arms lifting him to the ground. 'Mayer . . . get Mayer . . . mind his leg,' he muttered weakly. Then darkness surged up and around him as he fell into a sleep of utter exhaustion.

II

When he awoke the sun was throwing oblique shafts of yellow light through the gaps in the half-drawn curtains of his room. For a little while he saw them without understanding what they were, but as wakefulness cast out the last vestiges of sleep, he sat up with a yawn and stretched.

'So here we are again,' he thought, glancing round and noting that nothing appeared to have been touched. His hand came in contact with his chin and he started, but then smiled as he rubbed the stubble ruefully. He jumped out of bed, threw back the blinds, and surveyed himself in the mirror. 'Very pretty,' he muttered. 'A comely youth withal. Gosh! what a scallywag I look. I'm no oil painting at any time, but goodness me! I didn't think I could look quite such a scarecrow.'

119

That may have been taking rather a hard view, but his appearance was certainly anything but prepossessing. Two days' growth of sparse bristles on his chin formed a fitting background for a nasty cut in his lower lip, which was badly swollen, while his right eye was surrounded by a pale greenish-blue halo that did nothing to improve matters. A scratch across the forehead on which the blood had dried completed the melancholy picture. 'I'd better start work on myself,' he thought, reaching for his razor.

An orderly appeared while he was in the bath, and finding he was up, speedily returned with breakfast on a tray, and a broad smile which suggested to Biggles that he was in the Squadron's good books.

The Count arrived, beaming, while he was dressing, and after congratulating him on his rescue of Mayer, startled him by announcing in a grandiose voice that he had recommended him for the Iron Cross.

'It was not worth such an honour,' protested Biggles uncomfortably, for the idea of being decorated by the enemy did not fill him with enthusiasm. 'How is Mayer, by the way?'

'As well as one might expect, considering everything. The wound in his head is nothing, but his leg will take some time to get right. He has been awake a long time, and I have been with him; he had to wait for the ambulance to take him to the hospital in Jerusalem. While we waited he told me the story of what happened, or as much as he knows of it. How did you come to be taken prisoner in the first place?'

'I ran into a sandstorm and was forced down,' replied Biggles truthfully. 'I waited for the storm to pass, and was just getting back into my machine when a party of Arabs turned up and carted me off to the nearest

120

British post, where they held me to ransom, or sold me—or something of the sort.'

The Count frowned. 'They're unreliable these Arabs,' he said. 'I wouldn't trust them an inch. They betray either side for a handful of piastres and would cut the throat of every white man in the country if they could, or if they dared. Von Stalhein thinks a lot of them though, perhaps because he was out here before the war and knows their habits and language. That's why he's here now. Between ourselves, he's got a big show on at this very moment which—which—' He broke off abruptly as if he realized suddenly that he was saying too much. 'Come along down to the Mess as soon as you're ready,' he continued, changing the subject, as he moved towards the door. 'I want you to meet Kurt Hess.'

'Kurt Hess? I seem to have heard the name. Who is he?'

'He's our crack pilot in the East. He has scored twenty-six victories and is very proud of it, which is pardonable. He arrived this morning; he's only here for a few days, and between ourselves—' the Count dropped his voice to a confidential whisper—'he's not very pleased because every one is talking about you, and your exploit with Mayer. Perhaps he thinks, not unnaturally, that they should be talking about him.'

'I see,' answered Biggles as he brushed his tunic, and made a mental note that if he knew anything about German character he would find a ready-made enemy in the German Ace. 'I shall be proud to meet him,' he went on slowly, wondering what the Count would say if he knew that his own bag of enemy machines exceeded that of the German's.

'See you presently, then,' concluded the Count, as he went out and closed the door.

'So von Stalhein *is* leading the Arabs,' thought Biggles, 'and he isn't back yet. Well, I hope he gets it in the neck; it would save me a lot of trouble.' But even as the thought crossed his mind there was a roar overhead and a Halberstadt side-slipped steeply to a clever landing; it swung round and raced tail up towards the sheds. Before it had stopped, von Stalhein, in German uniform, had climbed out of the back seat and was limping quickly towards headqarters.

'It looks to me as if we might soon be hearing some interesting news,' mused Biggles, with a thrill of anticipation, as he went out and strolled towards the Mess.

Chapter 12
A New Pilot—And a Mission

I

There was no need to wonder which of the assembled officers was Hess. Holding the floor in the centre of an admiring group was a tall, slim, middle-aged man from whose throat hung the coveted Pour le Mérite, the highest award for valour in the German Imperial Forces. His manner and tone of voice were at once so haughty—one might say imperious—and supercilious, that Biggles, although he was half prepared for something of the sort, instinctively recoiled. 'What amazing people the Huns are,' he thought, as he watched the swaggering gestures of the Ace. 'Fancy any one of our fellows behaving like that and getting away with it. Why, he'd be slung out on his ear into the nearest pig-trough, and quite right, too. What an impossible sort of skunk he must be; yet here are all these fellows kow-towing to him as if he were an object for reverence just because he has had the luck to shoot down a few British machines. I doubt if he has ever run up against any one really hot; he'd soon get the dust knocked out of his pants if he was sent to France, I'll warrant.'

He walked across and stood on the outskirts of the group, listening respectfully, but the conversation was, of course, in German, so he could not follow it very well. He picked up a word or two here and there, however, sufficient for him to judge that the German was enlarging upon the simplicity of killing Englishmen when once one had the knack, for they had neither courage nor ability.

In spite of himself Biggles was amused at the man's overweening conceit, and his thoughts must have found expression on his face, for the German suddenly broke off in the middle of a sentence and scowled in a manner so puerile and affected that it was all Biggles could do to prevent himself from laughing out loud.

With the air of a king accepting homage from minions, the Ace moved slowly through the group until he stood face to face with the object of his disapproval; then with his lip curled in a sneer he said something quickly in German that Biggles did not understand. That it was something unpleasant he could feel from the embarrassed manner of the other Germans present.

Biggles glanced around the group calmly. 'Will some gentleman kindly tell him that I do not understand?' he said quietly in English.

But an interpreter was unnecessary. 'So!' said the Ace, in the same language, with affected surprise. 'What have we here—an Engländer?'

'He is of the Intelligence Staff,' put in Schmidt, who was Mayer's usual observer, and may have been prompted by a feeling of gratitude for what Biggles had done for his pilot. 'He's the officer who brought Mayer back last night.'

'So!' sneered Hess, with a gesture so insolent that Biggles itched to strike him. 'We know what to do with Engländers, we of the Hess *Jagdstaffel** Perhaps you

---

* A hunting group of German fighters, consisting of approximately twelve aeroplanes. Also just called a 'staffel'. The equivalent of a British squadron.

would like to hear how I make them sizzle in their seats,' he continued, addressing Biggles directly. 'I myself have shot down twenty-six—twenty-six—' he repeated the number, presumably to make sure that there could be no mistake—'like this.' He went through what was intended to be a graphic demonstration of the art of air fighting, but to Biggles it was merely comical. 'Twenty-six,' said Hess yet again, 'and by to-night it will be twenty-seven,' he added, 'for to-day is my birthday, and I have sworn not to sleep until I have sent another down like roast beef in his own oven.'

Biggles was finding it hard to keep his temper, for he knew that to fall out with the German idol would mean serious trouble. 'Excellent, *mein Hauptmann,*' he said, 'but take care you don't meet one that turns your own "box" into a coffin instead, for what would the Fatherland do without you?' The sarcasm which he could not veil was quite lost on the German, but it was not overlooked by one or two of the others, who stirred uncomfortably.

The Ace drew himself up to his full height and struck a pose. 'Do you suggest that an Engländer might shoot *me* down?' he inquired haughtily.

'There's just a chance, you know,' replied Biggles easily, clenching and unclenching his hands in his pockets. 'The English have some good fighters in France, and one may come out here one day. After all, were not Immelmann and Boelcke—'

'Zut! they were foolish,' broke in the Ace, with a movement of his arm that was probably intended to convey regret, but at the same time a suggestion of contempt, as if they were not in the same category as Kurt Hess.

Just where the matter would have ended it is impossible to say, but fortunately at that moment the Count, accompanied by von Stalhein, came into the room. One glance at their faces told Biggles all that he wanted to know about the Arab attack. That it had failed was certain, for the Count looked worried, while von Stalhein was pale under his tan and wore a bandage on his left hand.

The Count turned to speak to Hess while von Stalhein beckoned to Biggles, who walked over quickly to where the German was waiting for him.

'Count von Faubourg has just told me about the business of Mayer,' began von Stalhein abruptly. 'From what I gather, you put up a remarkably fine performance. Can you remember exactly where Mayer's machine crashed?'

'I think I can mark the position to within a mile or two, but Mayer was flying, not me, so I couldn't guarantee to be absolutely correct,' replied Biggles, wondering what was coming.

'Do you think you could find the crash?'

'Oh yes, there should be no difficulty about that.'

'Good! Then I want you to fly over and drop an incendiary bomb on the wreck. You must set it on fire with a direct hit, otherwise there is no point in going. The machine must be utterly destroyed. Do you think you could manage it?'

'I'm quite sure of it,' returned Biggles quickly, looking out of the window so that the other could not see the satisfaction in his eyes for the mission presented an opportunity for which he was anxiously waiting.

'Very well. Then get off at once; and will you please take a camera with you? To satisfy myself I should like to see a photograph—'

'Do you doubt my word, sir?' asked Biggles with an air of injured innocence.

'No, but important matters are at stake, and the only

way to be quite sure of a thing is to see it with one's own eyes.'

'I understand,' replied Biggles. 'I'll take a Pfalz and go over immediately.' He bowed and left the room and, collecting his overalls and flying kit from his room, made his way to the tarmac. As he walked along to the hangars of the Pfalz Squadron he stopped for a moment to look at a new scarlet and white Pfalz D. III Scout, around which a number of mechanics were standing, lost in admiration, for it was the latest product of the famous Pfalz works and far and away the best thing they had ever turned out. There was no aircraft in the Middle East to touch it for speed and climb, and to Biggles, who knew something of the value of these qualities in a fighting aeroplane, the chief reason for the successes of the German Ace was made clear—for he had no doubt to whom the Pfalz belonged.

There was a strange, ruminating look in his eyes as he walked on to the Pfalz Squadron, and asked if he could have a machine for a special mission. On being answered in the affirmative, he requested that four twenty-pound incendiary bombs be fitted to the bomb racks, and in a few minutes, with these in place, he taxied out and took off in the direction of his previous day's adventure.

II

He found plenty to occupy his mind as he cruised watchfully towards the place where the remains of the unfortunate Halberstadt were piled up, but the two chief matters that exercised his thoughts were von Stalhein's anxiety to secure the destruction of the machine, and the possibility of having a word with Algy.

As far as the crashed machine was concerned, it seemed certain that it contained something of importance, something that von Stalhein did not want to leave lying about, possibly a document of some sort. 'Obviously, I shall have to try to find out what it is before I start the bonfire,' he decided. 'I'd better attend to that first, and then go on to Abba Sud afterwards to see if Algy is still hanging about.'

He found the crash without difficulty, and after circling round for a few minutes looking for the best landing place, finally selected a patch free from rocks and camel-thorn, about half a mile away; it was the nearest place where he could get down without taking risks that he preferred to avoid. Leaving the propeller ticking over, he hastened to the well-remembered scene, and began a systematic search of the wreckage. At first he concentrated on the battered pilot's cockpit, going through all the pockets in turn; but they yielded nothing. For half an hour he hunted, and then, just as he was about to abandon the quest, thinking that perhaps after all von Stalhein was simply concerned with the destruction of the machine, he came upon an article so incongruous that he regarded it in stupefied amazement. He found it in what had evidently been a secret stowage place between the two cockpits, but the cavity had been burst open by the crash, revealing what lay within. It was a British officer's field service cap. There was nothing to show to whom it belonged, but the maker's name was that of a well-known London outfitter.

'Well, I don't know what I expected to find, but if I'd been given a thousand guesses I should never have guessed *that*,' thought Biggles, as he turned the cap over and over in his hands. 'But all the same, that must be the thing that friend Erich was scared about; or is

128

it simply a souvenir? It's no use burning a good hat, so I'll take it with me. And I might as well make sure of setting the crash alight, in case I miss it with my bombs,' he went on, as he took out a box of matches, struck one and held it to the sun-dried fabric. When it was well alight he ran back to his machine, took off, and dropped his bombs on the conflagration. Then he took two or three photographs of the fire with the oblique camera that he had brought for the purpose; still not entirely satisfied, he waited for a few minutes until the destruction of the machine was clearly revealed, when he took another photograph, and then raced off in the direction of the oasis of Abba Sud.

He saw Algy afar off long before he reached the oasis, a tiny speck in the sky that circled round and round the dark belt of trees, and presently resolved itself into an aeroplane of unorthodox design. The straight top plane, and lower ones set at a pronounced angle, could not belong to any other machine than a Sopwith Camel. At first Biggles could hardly believe his eyes as it came towards him, and he stared at it wonderingly. He fired a red Very light, the prearranged signal, to ensure that there should be no mistake, and his first words, as he jumped from his cockpit and ran towards the other machine that had landed near him, were, 'Algy! where did you get that kite?'

'Never mind about that; where the dickens have you been all this time?' growled Algy. 'I've been frizzling here like a herring in a pan for the last two blinking days. I was just beginning to think that the Huns must have shot you.'

'I've been busy,' retorted Biggles. 'Do you think I've nothing to do but chase to and fro between Zabala and here? I repeat, where did you get that Camel?'

'It's a special one that's been sent up for head-

129

quarters use. Fellows were beginning to grouse because a Hun—Hess, we hear his name is—is playing Old Harry up and down the lines with one of the Pfalz D. III's, and we've nothing to get near him in.'

'So I believe. I was talking to Hess this morning. The Huns think he's a prize piece of furniture, but, as a matter of fact, he's the prince of all swine.'

'Well, we got a Camel up from Heliopolis, and it's been handed over to me *pro tem*.,' went on Algy. 'I shot down a Halberstadt yesterday.'

Biggles started and his eyes narrowed. 'Where?' he asked coldly.

'About twenty miles to the north-east of where we are now. It hit the floor a dickens of a crack and went to pieces.'

'You needn't tell me: I was in it,' Biggles told him, grimly.

'You were—Oh, great Scott! Well, I wasn't to know that, was I? Why didn't you fire a red light?'

'A fat lot of chance you gave me. I didn't even see you until you started pumping out lead.'

'Of course; I didn't think of that. My word! I might have killed you.'

'Might! You thundering nearly did.'

'Well, I wasn't to know. I saw a Hun and I went for him. It didn't occur to me that you might be in it, because I thought you were wandering about behind the British lines.'

Biggles looked perplexed. 'How the deuce did you know that?' he demanded.

'Because sometime about midnight young Fraser, the lad who is in charge of Number Five post, rang up headquarters to say that he had collected a Hun prisoner named Brunow from a bunch of Arabs and wanted to know what he was to do with him. Headquarters told him to hang on to him until the morning and then send him along. Then they sent out the usual chit to Intelligence people asking if they wanted to interrogate him. Poor old Raymond nearly threw a fit when he heard it was you. He sent for me in a hurry, and at the first crack of dawn I went up with special instructions to fly you down to Kantara, but when I got there I found you'd already left in charge of a party of Major Sterne's Arabs who—'

'*Whose* Arabs?' Biggles fired the question like a pistol shot.

'Sterne's—why, what's wrong?'

Biggles looked at him oddly. 'Was Sterne up there when you got there?' he asked quietly.

'No, he'd just gone; pushed off out into the desert on one of his trips.'

Biggles stared and said nothing for a moment. 'Go on,' he murmured at last.

'Well, I went back to report what had happened, and in the afternoon the Arabs rolled up with a tale of how you'd escaped,' continued Algy.

'How had I escaped?'

'By jumping on the best horse while you were all resting, and leaping a terrific chasm over which it was impossible to follow you. They fired at you but missed, and then you disappeared behind some rocks and were never found again.'

'So, that's what they told you, is it?' mused Biggles. 'My gosh! what a tale. Makes those yarns about the Arabian Nights sound tame. I expect you got quite a kick out of it.'

'Why, didn't you bolt?'

'Bolt, my foot. But I haven't time to tell you the whole story now. Mayer, one of our Huns at Zabala, picked me up, and we were on our way back when you

131

butted in and shot us down. Mayer got a crack on the side of the nut from one of your bullets, but he wasn't dead, so I dragged him to an oasis where I saw a big bunch of Arabs collecting. I'd got a machine there—don't ask me how or why—so I flew down to Kantara to let you know what was going on. Did you get my message?'

'We certainly did. The telephone wires were red hot for a bit, I can tell you, and a whole lot of troops, mostly Australian cavalry, lost their beauty sleep. When the Sheikhs rolled up they were waiting for them, and they gave them such a plastering that they're not likely to forget in a hurry. Some got killed and some got away, but a lot were taken prisoners, and they're bleating for the blood of the man who led them into the trap, for that's what they swear happened. When—'

'I see. That clears things up a bit,' interrupted Biggles. 'I begin to see daylight. By the way, did you see the waterworks blow up when you were over Zabala the other night?'

Algy laughed. 'Too true I did,' he cried. 'What a wizard it was! I hooted like a coot in spite of the archie.'

'You reported it when you got back?'

'Of course. Our people were tickled to death, although they still don't know who did it, or how it was done. Raymond is as dumb as a church mouse.'

'I'm glad he is,' declared Biggles. 'And what about that news you had for me—the news you mentioned in the message you dropped?'

'Oh yes! I've been waiting to tell you about that. Raymond got a direct dispatch, in code, from London,. The Air Board told him that if possible he was to warn you to beware of Brunow.'

'Brunow! What the dickens has he got to do with it? He's in London.'

'No, he isn't. Something must have happened in London, and although our people were watching him like a cat watching a mouse, he disappeared suddenly as if he'd got the wind up, and they fancy it was something to do with you. They traced him as far as Hull, and then lost track of him, but they think he departed for Germany hot foot, via Holland. They thought you ought to be warned, in case he turned up here.'

'Why should he?'

'Don't ask me; I don't know.'

'I see.'

'Look! There's one last thing,' went on Algy. 'We've laid out a dummy aerodrome, twelve miles south-east of Kantara. It looks fine from the air. If you want to please the Huns and at the same time would like to see them waste some bombs, you can tell them where it is. It's all ready, fairly aching to be bombed,' he concluded with a broad grin.

'That's fine,' Biggles walked over and took the officer's cap that he had found in Mayer's cockpit from the back seat of his machine and handed it to Algy. 'Hang on to that,' he said. 'Take it back to Raymond when you go and tell him to hide it—bury it if he likes. He can do what he likes with it, but on no account must any one see it. Got that?'

'Yes. That's quite clear.'

'Good! Now lend me that Camel for half an hour. You can wait here for me; I'll bring it back.'

Algy's jaw dropped. 'Lend you the Camel?' he gasped.

'That's what I said,' returned Biggles. 'What are you gaping at; is it an unnatural request?'

'Er—no. But what do you want it for?'

'Because I've a strong urge to be myself for a few minutes.'

'Be yourself? What are you talking about? Have you got a touch of sun or something?'

'My goodness! You are dense this morning. I just have a feeling that I'd like to forget that I'm Brunow for a little while and be what I am—a junior officer in the R.F.C.'

'But what for?'

Biggles looked exasperated. 'All right, if you *must* know,' he said slowly and deliberately. 'There's a fellow floating about the atmosphere in a red and white Pfalz D. III who thinks he's cock of the roost. He's promised to fry his twenty-seventh Englishman to-day—the conceited ass—and when I saw your Camel it struck me that it wouldn't be a bad scheme if I took a hand in this frying business.'

'You mean Hess.'

'Yes rhymes with Hess, and so does mess, which is as it should be,' observed Biggles, 'because I'm going to do my best to get Mr. Hess in the biggest mess he was ever in. Are these guns O.K.?'

'Perfectly O.K.'

'Then give me a swing.'

Algy ran to the propeller. The engine sprang into life, and the Camel sped across the desert like a blunt-nosed bullet with the slipstream hurling a cloud of sand high into the air behind it.

Chapter 13
Vickers Versus Spandaus

In his heart Biggles knew that from the first moment he saw the swaggering German Ace the greatest ambition of his life was to see him given the lesson he so richly deserved, the lesson which would inevitably be administered sooner or later by somebody; and he had resolved to set about the task that morning in the Pup he assumed Algy would be flying. That his partner was, in fact, flying a Sopwith Camel was better luck than he could have imagined, for it evened things up.

Previously, in a Pfalz D.III, Hess could choose his own battle-field and select his opponent, for in the event of his catching a foeman who turned out to be a tartar, he could break off the combat and escape by virtue of his superior speed. This advantage of superior equipment was the dominating factor that enabled many German Aces to pile up big scores during certain periods of 1916 and 1917, a lamentable state of affairs that came to a sudden end with the arrival at the front of the Camel and the S.E.5, as the appalling death roll of German Aces towards the end of 1917 reveals.

Sopwith Camels had been in France, where the fighting was most intense, for some time, but none had reached the outlying theatres of war; consequently, a German pilot arriving in one of the distant battle-fields with the latest German fighting machine, finding himself opposed to aeroplanes of obsolete type, had every opportunity of acquiring a reputation that was often proved to be false when he encountered opponents on level terms.

But with these matters Biggles was not concerned as he sped towards the German side of the battlefield, which he knew would be the most likely place to find the German Ace lying in wait for a British two-seater; and he was jubilant at once more finding himself in the cockpit of a Camel for two reasons. In the first place he was thoroughly at home, and secondly he would be able to force the German to fight, provided he found him, for the simple reason that he would not be able to run away, as the two machines were about equal in performance.

He might, of course, have shot the German down from his own Pfalz, but the thought did not occur to him, for it would have been little short of murder; he felt that in a regular British aircraft he was perfectly justified in fighting Hess. He would forget for the moment that he had ever existed as Brunow, and behave precisely as if he had been posted to the Middle East as an ordinary pilot of a fighter squadron. In those circumstances the combat, if it occurred, would be perfectly fair.

He reached the lines but could see no signs of aerial activity, so climbing steadily for height, he began a systematic search of the whole sector. Once he saw a Halberstadt in the distance but he ignored it, for it was not the object of his quest, and he continued on his way, eyes probing the skies above and below for the red and white fuselage of the Pfalz. A little later he passed close to an antiquated B.E.2 C* and exchanged

* Designed in 1912 for observation and artillery co-operation this two-seater biplane whose top speed of 72 mph was just half that of the fastest fighters, was clearly obsolete by 1918.

greetings with its crew, at the same time admiring their courage for taking the air in a conveyance so hopelessly out of date. 'That's the sort of kite Hess is hoping to meet, I'll bet; and if he could poke in a burst of fire without being seen he'd be tickled to death; probably go back to Zabala and tell the boys how easy it is to shoot down Englishmen,' he mused. 'Pah! Well, we'll see.'

He had flown on for some little distance and was scanning the sky ahead when something—possibly the instinct which experienced air fighters seemed to develop—made him look back long and searchingly at the B.E., now a speck in the eastern sky. Was it his imagination, or was there a tiny speck moving far above it? He closed his eyes for a moment and then looked again, forcing them to focus in spite of the glare; then he caught his breath sharply and swung the Camel round in the lightning right-hand turn that was one of its most famous characteristics. He had not been mistaken. Far above the plodding B.E. a minute spark of light had flashed for a brief instant. No one but an old hand would have seen it or known what it portended; but Biggles knew that it was the sun's rays catching the wings of a banking aeroplane.

A minute or two later he could see it clearly as it stalked its quarry from the cover of the sun's blinding glare; he could see from its shape that it was a Pfalz, but it was still too far off for him to make out its colours. 'No matter,' he thought; 'I shall have to give those two boys in the B.E. the tip, whether it's Hess or not, or else it looks like being their unlucky day.'

He was flying rather higher than the German scout, which in turn was some distance above the slow two-seater, and his advantage of height gave him the extra speed necessary to come up with them. While he was

137

still half a mile away his lips parted in the grim smile he always wore when he was fighting as he picked out the colours of the Pfalz. They were red and white. It had placed itself in an ideal position for attack, and its nose was already going down to deliver the thrust that would send the British two-seater to its doom.

Biggles shoved his joystick forward savagely, and the needle of his air speed indicator swung upwards to the one hundred and eighty miles an hour mark; but he did not see it, for his eyes were glued on the now diving scout. He snatched a glance downwards and saw the gunner of the B.E. leaning over the side of his cockpit, looking down at the ground and making notes in a writing-pad, unconscious of the hand of death that was falling on him from the skies.

Biggles was afraid he was going to be too late, so he took the only course open to him; his hand closed over the firing lever of his guns and he fired a long deflexion* shot in the direction of the Hun, more with the object of calling attention to himself than in any real hope of hitting it. Hess apparently did not hear the shots, for he continued his swoop, but the British pilot did, and acted with admirable presence of mind. He glanced up, not at the Pfalz but in the direction from which the rattle of guns had come, and saw the Camel. Whether he suspected that the British pilot had mistaken him for a Hun, or whether he felt the presence of some unseen danger, Biggles never knew, but he turned sharply, so sharply that his gunner fell back into his seat with alarm as he reached for his gun.

The action was quite enough to disconcert the Pfalz pilot, who may have suspected a trap, for he swerved

* The amount a gunner or pilot must aim ahead of a fast moving aircraft, passing at right angles, in order to hit it.

wildly and careered round in a wide circle, looking over his shoulder for the cause of the B.E. pilot's manœuvre. It was a foolish move, and at once betrayed the man's lack of real ability, for Biggles swept down on him and could have fired a burst which might well have ended the combat there and had he been so inclined. But this was not his intention. Moved by some impulse altogether foreign to his nature and his usual methods of fighting, he roared down alongside Pfalz, passing it so closely that their wing tips almost touched. As he passed he tore off his helmet and goggles, flung them on the floor of the cockpit, and stared with smouldering eyes into the face of the German. There was no smile on his own face now, but a burning hatred of the man who shot down machines of inferior performance and then boasted of his prowess. He saw the look of recognition spring into the German's eyes, and the fear that followed it. 'Not so sure of yourself now, are you?' snarled Biggles. 'Come on, you skunk—fight!'

With a savage exaltation that he had never known before, he whirled round, and nearly collided with the B.E. which, with the best intentions, had decided to take a hand. For a moment he saw red. 'Get out of my way, you fool,' he raged, uselessly as he tilted his wing, and missing the B.E. by inches, gave its pilot the shock of his life.

The moves had lost him two seconds of time, and before he was on even keel again the Pfalz had got a lead of a quarter of a mile, and was racing, nose down, for home. 'Not so fast, my cock,' growled Biggles, as he stood on the rudder and shoved the stick forward. What happened to the B.E. after that he did not know, for he never saw it again. He sent a stream of tracer down the slipstream of the red and white machine, and sneered as the pilot swerved away from it, regardless of the fact that at such a range the odds were a thousand to one against a hit.

'You cold-footed rabbit; what about the frying you were so anxious about this morning?' muttered Biggles, as he closed the gap that separated them and sewed a line of leaden stitches down the red and white fuselage. The German swung round with the desperate courage born of despair and sprayed a triple* line of bullets at his relentless pursuer; but Biggles touched his rudder-bar lightly and side-slipped away, whereupon Hess, acknowledging his master, cut his engine and began to slip towards the ground.

'You're not getting away with that, you rat,' grated Biggles, blazing up with fury at such a craven display. 'If you want to go down, then go, and I'll help you on your way,' he snarled, as he roared down on the tail of the falling Ace. He held his fire until his propeller was a few feet from the blackcrossed rudder, and then pressed the gun lever. A double line of orange flame leapt from his engine cowling. To Biggles' atonishment, the German made no effort to defend himself. For a fraction of a second he looked back over his shoulder and read his fate in the spouting muzzles of the twin Vickers guns; then he slumped forward in his cockpit. A tiny tongue of flame curled aft from the scarlet petrol tank; it grew larger and larger until it was a devouring furnace that dropped through the air like a stone.

Biggles pulled out of his dive and turned away feeling suddenly sick, as he often did when he sent down an enemy machine in flames; when he looked back a great cloud of black smoke, towards which tiny figures were running, marked the funeral pyre of the man who had

* Some models of the Pfalz DIII were fitted with three Spandau machine guns, synchronised to fire through the propeller.

sworn to fry an Englishman as his own birthday present.

'I might as well get back,' he thought, glancing round the sky. The B.E. had disappeared, and there were no other machines in sight, so he set a course for the oasis, feeling tired and irritable now that his anger had burned itself out.

He found Algy examining the Pfalz with professional interest when he got back to Abba Sud.

'Any luck?' queried Algy, expectantly, as he walked towards him.

'You can call it luck if you like,' replied Biggles, simply, 'but Hess won't worry our fellows any more. Make out a combat report when you get back and put in a claim for a red and white Pfalz that fell in flames three miles north of Jebel Tire at 10.51 a.m. Our forward observation posts must have seen the show and will confirm it.

'I shall do nothing of the sort,' cried Algy indignantly; 'he was your meat.'

'I don't want the Huns to know that, do I, you ass?' snapped Biggles. 'You do what you're told. And remember, you don't know it's Hess. Our people will get that information from the other side in due course. That's all, laddie,' he went on with a change of tone. 'I must be getting back now.' He looked suddenly old and tired.

'O.K., Skipper,' replied Algy, looking at him under his lashes, and noting the symptoms of frayed nerves. 'When am I going to see you again?'

'I don't know,' muttered Biggles, 'but pretty soon, I hope. Tell Raymond that I'm running on a hot scent,' he went on wistfully, 'and I hope to be back in 266 Squadron again before the end of the month—or else—'

141

'Or else?' questioned Algy.

'Nothing.' Biggles looked Algy squarely in the eyes. 'Thank God it will soon be over one way or the other,' he said quietly. 'I wasn't made for this game, and I've had about enough. But I've got to go on—to the end—you see that, don't you, old lad?'

'Of course,' replied Algy, swallowing something in his throat.

'I thought you would. Well, cheerio, old boy.'

'Cheerio, old son.'

Their hands met in a firm grip, the only time during the whole war that either of them allowed their real feelings to get uppermost.

Algy stood beside the Camel and watched the Pfalz until it disappeared from sight. 'Those soulless hounds at the Air Board need boiling in oil for sending a fellow like Biggles on a job like this,' he muttered huskily. 'Still, I suppose it's what they call war,' he added, as he climbed slowly into his cockpit.

Chapter 14
Biggles Flies a Bomber

Biggles arrived back at Zabala just as the station was closing down work for lunch. He handed his camera to the photographic sergeant with instructions to be particularly careful with the negatives, and to bring him a print of each as quickly as possible, and he was walking down to the headquarters offices when he saw von Stalhein and the Count, who had evidently heard him land, waiting for him.

'Did you manage it all right?' inquired von Stalhein, with his eyes on Biggles' face.

'I burnt the machine and took the photographs, but naturally I can't say what they're like until I've seen them.'

'Did you land?' Von Stalhein asked the question sharply, almost as if his intention was to catch Biggles off his guard.

'Land!' replied Biggles with a puzzled frown. 'Why should I risk a landing in the desert when I had incendiary bombs with me?'

'Oh, I merely wondered if you had—just as a matter of interest,' retorted von Stalhein. 'You've been a long time, haven't you?'

'As a matter of fact, I have,' admitted Biggles. 'I intended going straight there and back, but I saw something that intrigued me and I thought it was worth while following it up.'

'Indeed! and what was it?' asked the Count, interestedly.

'A new type of British machine, sir,' answered Biggles. 'I didn't think they had any of them on this front; maybe they have only just arrived.'

'What sort of machine was it?'

'A very fast machine with no dihedral on the top plane; they call it the Camel, I think, and it's made at the Sopwith works.'

The Count grimaced. 'I've heard of them in France,' he said quickly. 'What did you do?'

'I took up a position in the sun and watched it, thinking it might possibly lead to the aerodrome of a new squadron.'

'Splendid! What then?'

'The machine crossed the British lines and began to glide down, so I climbed as high as my machine would take me and saw it land at what looks like a new aerodrome about twelve miles south-east of Kantara. I'm not sure about it being a new aerodrome because I haven't had time to verify it in the map-room; it may have been there a long time, but I've never noticed it before.'

'I've never heard of an aerodrome there,' declared the Count, while von Stalhein looked puzzled.

'It wasn't there a few days ago,' he said slowly.

Biggles wondered how he knew that, but said nothing.

'Very well, go in and get some lunch,' went on the Count. 'Our Brunow is becoming quite useful, eh, Erich?'

Von Stalhein smiled a curious smile that always gave Biggles a tingling feeling down the spine, but whatever his thoughts were he did not disclose them, so Biggles saluted and departed in the direction of the Mess.

He had just finished lunch when an orderly arrived with a message that he was wanted at headquarters, so he tossed his napkin on the table, swallowed the last drop of coffee in his cup, and with an easy mind made his way to the Count's office.

'Ah, Brunow, there you are,' began von Faubourg, who was sitting at his desk while von Stalhein leaned in his usual position against the side, blowing clouds of cigarette smoke into the air. 'We've been talking about this report of yours concerning the new aerodrome,' continued the Count, 'and we have decided that there is a strong probability that the British have brought out a new squadron, in which case it would be a good plan to let it know what to expect. If we can put some of the machines out of action so much the better, otherwise we're likely to have some casualties. I suppose you've heard that Hess hasn't come back from his morning patrol? We don't take the matter seriously, but I've rung up the other squadrons who say that they have seen nothing of him, so it rather looks as if he had forced landed somewhere.'

Biggles nodded. 'That must be the case, sir. One can hardly imagine him coming to any harm,' he said seriously.

'No, the thought is preposterous. But about this projected bomb raid. You marked down the exact position of the aerodrome, did you not?'

'I did, sir.'

'I thought I understood you to say that. I've detailed six machines to go over this afternoon and strike while the iron is hot, so to speak, and in order that there should be no mistake I want you to fly the leading one.'

Biggles started. 'You want me to lead the bombers, sir?' he ejaculated.

'Why not? It is a trifle irregular, I know, and Ober-

145

leutnant* Kranz, who is commanding the *Staffel* in Mayer's absence, may feel hurt about it, but as you know where the place is you will be able to go straight to it. Kranz can still be in command, but you could show the way and take charge of the operation just while you were over the British lines. Is that quite clear?'

'Quite, sir,' replied Biggles, whose head was in a whirl at this fresh complication. The idea that he might have to accompany a raid, much less lead one, had not occurred to him.

'Each machine will carry two heavy bombs,' continued the Count, 'and one machine will, of course, take a camera so that we can study the layout of the aerodrome at our leisure as well as see if the bombs do any damage.'

'I'll take the camera if you like, sir,' volunteered Biggles, who thought he might as well be hung for a sheep as a lamb.

'That would be excellent. Then I'll leave it to you to fix up the details with Kranz. Good luck!'

Biggles saluted and withdrew with mixed feelings, for the fact that the dummy aerodrome lure had worked out well was rather overshadowed by the part that he had been detailed to play, and he realized that during the next two hours there was a strong possibility that he would be shot down by his own countrymen; and he did not overlook the fact that in the event of his formation being attacked, he might find it difficult not to put up some sort of fight, or pretence of fighting, yet he had no desire to be responsible for the death of a British pilot.

'I shall have to hope for the best, that's all there is

* Flying Officer in the German Air Force

to it,' he thought as he walked along to the hangars where the bustle indicated that preparations for the raid were going forward.

Half an hour later the six machines left the ground in V-formation with Biggles flying at the spear-head, and climbed steeply for altitude. For nearly an hour they roared upwards on a broad zigzag course before heading straight for the lines. They crossed over through a thin and futile archie barrage, and then raced on full throttle towards the now visible aerodrome.

Biggles, who, of course, had not seen it before, was completely amused at the realism of the bait. It was complete in every detail, even to some machines standing on the tarmac. There was no wind so it was unneccesary to turn in order to deliver the attack, and the first six bombs sailed down. But to Biggles' disgust they nearly all went wide; one only fell on the aerodrome and none touched any of the buildings. He had hoped to take a really thrilling photograph back to the Count, showing at least one hangar in flames.

The six machines turned slowly in a wide circle in order not to lose formation, and then returning from the opposite direction, laid their remaining eggs, that is, all except Biggles, who was determined to score a hit, for now that he was actually engaged in the task, the idea of bombing a British aerodrome amused him.

This time the aim was better. Two bombs fell on the aerodrome, and one in the end hangar, but still he was not satisfied, so he dived out of formation, losing height as quickly as possible, and turning again towards the aerodrome, took the centre buildings in his bomb-sight and pulled the toggle. For a few seconds the bomb diminished in size in a remarkable manner as it plunged earthwards, and then a pillar of smoke and flame leapt high into the air. It was a direct hit. He had his

147

camera over the side in an instant, but the movement might almost have been a signal, for he had only taken two photographs when such a tornado of archie burst around him that he dropped the instrument quickly on to the floor of the cockpit and pulled up his nose to rejoin the formation.

The other five machines were in no better case, and it seemed to him as he raced through a sea of smoke and flame that every anti-aircraft gun on the British front had been concentrated on the spot.

'Of course they have: what a fool I am,' he swore. 'Raymond would know that I'd give the Huns the position of the aerodrome, in which case it would be certain that sooner or later a formation of Boche bombers would come over. He could easily get the guns together without disclosing anything about my part of the business. My gosh! I ought to have thought of that.' He flinched as a piece of metal tore through his wing and made the machine vibrate from nose to rudder. A shell burst under his tail, and his observer, a youth named Bronveld, made desperate signals to him to get out of the vicinity as soon as possible.

He needed no urging. His one idea at that moment was to remove himself with the utmost possible speed from the hornets' nest he had stirred up, and all the time he was wondering what the other pilots would say, and more important still, what the Count would say when they got back—if they did—for the whole exploit bore a suspicious likeness to a well-laid trap. 'No,' he reasoned, as he side-slipped away from a well-placed bracket* that blossomed out in front of him, 'they can't blame me very well, for after all, I'm in the show myself, and no one is fool enough to step into a

---

* Bursting shells on both sides of a target

trap they have themselves set. In fact, it begins to look almost as if it were a good thing that I came on the show, otherwise—'

His high speed soliloquy was cut short by an explosion under his wing tip that nearly turned him upside down. He tried the controls with frantic haste, and breathed a prayer of thankfulness when he found that they were still functioning, but a long strip of fabric that trailed aft from his lower starboard plane made him feel uneasy. One of the other machines suddenly dipped its nose and began gliding down; he noted that its propeller had stopped, but thought it might just manage to reach the German lines that now loomed up ahead of them.

The formation, which had become badly scattered in the barrage, now began to re-form, and he had just taken his place in the lead when, glancing forward through the centre-section, he saw something that set his finger-tips tingling. Cutting across their front on a course that would effectually cut them off from the German lines were two squadrons of aeroplanes that needed no second look to identify them. One squadron, approaching from the west, was composed of eight Sopwith Pups with a solitary Camel hanging on its flank; the other, which was coming up from the east, comprised six Bristol Fighters.

Biggles eyed the Camel with a strange expression on his face, for the circumstances were so—well, he didn't know quite what to call them, for never before had he seen comedy and imminent tragedy so hopelessly intermingled. 'I'd bet a month's pay to a piastre that Algy has a smack at me first; he always does like taking on the leader,' he muttered. 'And I'd have won,' he went on bitterly, as the Camel pulled up in a steep

149

zoom, half-rolled, and then whirled round for the attack with its nose pointing down at Biggles' Halberstadt.

For once Biggles was nonplussed and a thousand ideas flashed through his brain, only to be abandoned instantly as he realized their uselessness. He glanced back over his shoulder and saw Bronveld crouching over his gun, waiting for the Camel to come within range. The lad's face was grim and set, but his hands were steady, and Biggles felt a thrill of apprehension. 'That kid's going to put up a good fight,' he thought anxiously. 'And from the way Algy is handling that Camel it looks to me as if the young fool stands a good chance of stopping a packet of Spandau bullets. He must be crazy to come down on top of us like that, straight over our rear gun.'

Then something like panic seized him as he visualized the unthinkable picture of his gunner killing Algy, or conversely, Algy's feelings when he found he had shot down his best friend. Whatever else happened, that must be avoided at all costs. Better to betray himself and be shot by the Huns than that should happen. 'At least I can let him know it's me,' he thought as, white-faced, he reached for his signal pistol, slipped in a red cartridge, and sent a streak of scarlet fire blazing across the nose of the diving Camel. But to his horror the pilot paid no attention to it, although, as if actuated by a common motive, the four remaining Halberstadts banked hard to the right and closed in on him. More with the object of avoiding a collision, he swung round in a fairly steep bank, and the other machines fell in line behind him.

The movement disconcerted the British pilots, who now found themselves facing an ever-circling ring from which guns spat every time they tried to approach, and while they were still milling round them in indecision,

Biggles darted out of the circle at a tangent and raced, nose down, for home. By the time the Pups and Bristols realized what had happened the other Halberstadts had followed on his tail and had established a clear lead, which they were able to keep until they were well inside their own territory. The danger was averted.

Biggles brushed his hand across his forehead. 'Phew! that was quite enough of that,' he muttered, as he looked back over his shoulder, and then stiffened with horror at the sight that met his eyes. The British machines, with the exception of one, had turned back, but the Camel, by reason of its superior speed, had continued the chase and had caught them. What was worse, its pilot was evidently still determined to strike at the leader of the Hun formation, and was roaring down in a final effort. As it came within range jets of orange flame darted from the muzzles of the guns on its engine cowling, and at the same moment, Bronveld, who was alive to the danger and crouching low behind his Parabellum gun, pulled the trigger. His aim was true. Biggles saw the tracer leap across the intervening space in a straight line that ended at the whirling engine of the British machine. Something stung his shoulder but he hardly felt it, for his eyes were fixed on the Camel in a kind of fascinated horror. Its nose had jerked up in a vertical zoom; for a moment it hung in space with its propeller threshing the air uselessly; then it turned slowly over on to its back and plunged earthward.

In a state of mental paralysis Biggles watched it hurtling through space. He couldn't think. He couldn't act. He could only stare ashen-faced at the spinning machine. He saw a wing break off, and the fuselage with its human cargo drop like a cannon-ball; then he turned away. He shifted his gaze to Bronveld, who was

151

clapping his hands jubilantly. As their eyes met the German showed his teeth in a victorious smile and turned his thumbs upwards, a signal that means the same thing the world over. Biggles could not find it in his heart to blame him, for it was the boy's first victory, and once, long ago, he had behaved in exactly the same way; only that time the spinning machine had black crosses on its wings, not red, white, and blue circles.

He turned back to his own cockpit feeling as if he had turned into a block of stone. Something seemed to have died inside him, leaving in its place only a bitter hatred of the war and everything connected with it. He ground his teeth under the emotion that shook him like a leaf, while in his mind hammered a single thought, 'Algy has gone west . . . Algy has gone west.' The wind seemed to howl it in the wires, and the deep-throated Mercedes engine purred it in a monotonous vibrating drone.

Through a shimmering atmosphere of unreality he saw the aerodrome at Zabala loom up, and automatically throttled back to land. His actions were purely instinctive as he flattened out and taxied slowly up to the hangars. The Count, von Stalhein, and several other officers were standing on the tarmac waiting, but none of them meant anything to him now. He no longer feared von Stalhein. He no longer cared a fig if he was suspected, arrested, or even shot.

He switched off, climbed stiffly to the ground, and walked slowly towards the spot upon which the others were converging. He could hear a babel of voices around him, German voices, and a wave of hatred swept over him. What was happening? He hardly knew. He became aware that Bronveld was tapping him on the back while he spoke rapidly to Faubourg. They were all laughing, talking over the battle, and a strange feeling swept over Biggles that he had seen it all before. Where had he seen the same thing? Suddenly he knew. The scene was precisely that which occurred on any British aerodrome after a raid; only the uniforms and the machines with the sinister Maltese crosses were different. As in a dream he heard the Count speaking.

'Splendid,' he was saying, 'splendid. Kranz is full of praise for the way you handled a nasty situation. Your firing of the red signal to form circle when you did, he says, saved the whole formation. And that last bomb of yours, and the way you left the formation to make sure of a hit, was brilliant. Your recommendation for the Iron Cross shall go off to-day. And Bronveld has shot down a Camel. We knew that before you got home; it fell in our lines and the artillery rang up to say they are sending the body here for burial. We will see that it is done properly, as we always do, because we know the British do the same for us. But what's this? Why! you're wounded, man.' He pointed to Biggles' shoulder, where a nasty-looking red stain was slowly spreading round a jagged tear in his overalls.

'Oh, that.' Biggles laughed, a hard, unpleasant sound. 'That's nothing. I hardly noticed it. The Camel fired the shot,' he added, wishing that it had gone through his head instead of his shoulder.

'While you were holding your machine steady so that Bronveld could shoot,' observed the Count. 'That is the sort of courage that will serve the *Vaterland*.* But go and get your shoulder attended to and make out your reports, all of you. I am looking forward to seeing the photographs.'

Biggles removed his flying cap and goggles and walked towards the Medical Officer's tent. He was

* The Fatherland: Germany

conscious that von Stalhein was watching him with the same puzzled expression that he had worn after the Mayer exploit. 'He doesn't know what to make of me,' he thought. 'Well, a fat lot I care what he thinks. I'll fly over to Raymond to-morrow, and throw my hand in; in future I'm flying in my own uniform, in France, or not at all. I've had enough of this dirty game and I never want to see a palm tree again.'

The wound, which was little more than a graze, was washed and bandaged by the elderly, good-natured German doctor, after which he went to his room and threw himself on his bed. The sun was sinking like a fiery orange ball in a crimson sky that merged into purple overhead, and threw a lurid glow on the hangars and the sentinel-like palms. It flooded into his room and bathed his bed, his uniform, and his tired face in a blood-red sheen.

For a long time he lay quite still, trying to think, trying to adjust himself to the new state of things, but in vain. His most poignant thought, the thing that worried him most, was the fact that he had been responsible for Algy's death in the first place by causing him to be posted from France to the land of the Israelites. That Algy might have been killed if he had remained in France did not occur to him. 'But there, what does it matter? What does anything matter? The lad's gone topsides, and that's the end of it,' he thought, as he rose wearily. He washed, and was drying his face, when an unusual sound took him to the window. A tender had stopped and half a dozen grey-coated soldiers in the uniform of the German Field Artillery, under the supervision of a Flying Corps officer, were unloading something. It was a long slim object shrouded in a dark blanket.

He watched with an expressionless face, for he was

past feeling anything. It was all a part of the scheme, the moving of the relentless finger of Fate that had lain over Palestine like a blight for nearly two thousand years and left a trail of death in its wake. He watched the soldiers carry the body into the tent that had been set aside as a temporary mortuary. He saw them come out, close the flap behind them, salute, and return to the tender, which, with a grinding of gears, moved slowly across the sand and disappeared from sight. It was like watching a scene in a play.

Then, moved by some impulse, he picked up his cap, left the room, and strode firmly towards the tent. 'I might as well say good-bye to the lad,' he thought, with his nostrils quivering. He threw aside the flap, entered, and stood in dumb misery at the end of the camp bed on which the pitiful object rested. Slowly and with a hand that shook, he lifted the end of the blanket—and looked.

How long he stood there he never knew. Time seemed to stand still. The deathly hush that falls over the desert at the approach of twilight had fallen; somewhere in the desert a sand-cricket was chirping. That was all. And still he stared—and stared.

At last, with a movement that was almost convulsive, he replaced the blanket, stepped back, and leaned against the tent-pole while he fought back an hysterical desire to laugh aloud—for the face was not Algy's. It was that of a middle-aged man in the uniform of an infantry regiment, with pilot's wings sewn on his tunic above the white and violet ribbon of the Military Cross. It was quite peaceful. A tiny blue hole above the left eyebrow showed where life had fled, leaving a faint smile of surprise on the countenance, so suddenly had the end come.

Biggles pulled himself together with a stupendous

155

effort and walked reverently from the presence of Death. With his teeth clenched, he hurried back to his room and flung himself face downwards on his bed, laughing and sobbing in turn. He did not hear the door open quietly to admit an orderly with tea on a tray, who, when his startled eyes fell on his superior officer, withdrew quickly and returned to the camp kitchen.

'Karl,' he called to the cook, 'Brunow's finished— nerve's gone to bits. Funny how all these flyers go the same in the end. Well, I don't care as long as they'll let me keep *my* feet on the ground.'

Chapter 15
Ordeal by Night

The German orderly, although he had good reason for thinking that 'Brunow's nerves had gone to bits', was far from right. Biggles' nerves were unimpaired, although it must be admitted that he had been badly shaken by the belief that Algy had been killed, but after the first reaction had spent itself the knowledge that the whole thing had been nothing more than a bad dream was such a relief that he prepared to resume his work with a greater determination than before. Lying propped up on his pillow, he reviewed the events of the day which, taking things all round, might have panned out a good deal worse. Hess had gone west, and he had no regrets on that score. 'Yes, taking it all round I've been pretty lucky to-day,' he mused, which was not strictly true, for such successes as he had achieved had been due more to clear thinking and ability than to good fortune. His only stroke of what could be regarded as luck was the firing of the red signal light which had saved the formation, thereby putting up his reputation with the *Staffel*, for when he had fired it he had not the remotest idea that it was the German signal to 'form circle', a fact that he could only assume was the case from what followed.

By dinner-time he was normal again but eager to see the end of his masquerade in order that he might return to normal duties. So deep-rooted was this longing that he was prepared to take almost any chance, regardless of risks, in order to expedite the conclusion of the affair.

Certain vital facts he had already grasped; of others, a shrewd suspicion was rapidly forming in his mind, and he only needed confirmation of them to send him to British headquarters and place his knowledge at the disposal of those who would know best how to act upon it.

It was with a determination born of these thoughts that he decided during dinner to pursue his quest in a manner which inwardly appalled him, but which, he thought, if successful could hardly fail to produce results. The idea came to him on the spur of the moment when he heard a machine taxi out across the aerodrome. Subconsciously he waited, expecting to hear it take off, but when it did not he knew—guessed would perhaps be a better word—that it was standing on the far side of the aerodrome waiting for a passenger about whose identity there was no doubt in his mind. And when a few minutes later von Stalhein left his chair, and after a whispered conversation with the Count, went out of the room, he fancied that he knew what was about to take place.

He would have liked to follow at once in order to watch von Stanhein, but that was out of the question, for it was a matter of etiquette that until the Count rose and led the way to the ante-room, no one could leave his place without asking his permission, and then a very good excuse would be demanded.

So he sat where he was, sipping his coffee, but listening for the sound that would denote von Stalhein's departure for the British lines; and he had not long to wait. Within a few minutes there came the distant roar of an aero engine; it swelled to a deep crescendo and then died away in the distance. 'There he goes,' he thought. 'If I could only be at the other end when he lands I might learn something.'

Now that his mind was made up on a course of action he fidgeted with impatience for the meal to end, and when at length the Count got up, the signal for a general move, he followed the others through to the ante-room with a light-heartedness which sprang, not from anticipation of the self-imposed undertaking before him, but from relief of knowing that the time had come to begin. He hung about conspicuously for a little while, turning over the pages of a magazine, and then satisfied that everyone was settling down for a quiet evening, he left the room and walked unhurriedly to his quarters, where he changed his regulation boots for a pair of the canvas shoes that most of the officers wore when off duty, and slipped an electric torch into his pocket. This done, he strolled towards the tarmac. He did not go as far as the front of the hangars, but turned to the left behind them and moved along in the direction of the fort. The building was in darkness, but knowing that a sentry would be on door duty, he kept to the rear, and then worked his way down the side until he stood under the window where, a few nights before, he had seen von Stalhein writing.

With his heart thumping in spite of his outward calm, he took a swift glance around to make sure that he was not being watched, and then, reaching for the window-sill, drew himself up until he could throw a leg across the wooden frame. The other followed, and he slipped quietly inside.

After the bright starlight outside he could see nothing at first, but by waiting a minute or two for his eyes to become accustomed to the darkness, he could just make out the general outlines of the furniture. He crossed swiftly to the door, and tried it, but as he expected, it was locked, so he went over to the writing-desk upon which a number of documents were lying, but they were, of course, written in German, so he did not touch them. In any case he was not particularly concerned with them. Working swiftly but quietly, he made a complete inspection of the room, and then turned to the tall wardrobe which stood against the far wall. He opened it, and shielding the torch with his cupped hands, he flashed it on the interior, when he heard a sound that brought him round with a start although not particularly alarmed, for it came from the direction of the window. It seemed to be a soft scraping noise, a rustling, as if a large bird had settled on the ledge.

Bending forward, he could just make out two dark objects that moved along the window-sill with a kind of groping movement. For a moment he could not make out what they were, and then he understood. They were hands. Some one was coming in through the window.

Now even in the flash of time that remained for him to think, he knew there were only two courses open to him. One was to step forward and confront the marauder, who, by his clandestine method of entry, obviously had no more right in the room than he had, and the other was to hide. Of the two the latter found more favour, for the very last thing he wanted was the hullabaloo that might conceivably take place if he allowed himself to be seen. So he stepped back, squeezed himself into the wardrobe, and pulled the door nearly shut behind him just as a man's head appeared in the square of star-spangled deep blue that marked the position of the window. Even in the uncertain light a single glance was sufficient to show that it was not a European, for the dark-bearded face was surmounted by a turban. As silent as a shadow, the Arab swung his legs and body over the sill with the feline grace of a panther, and stood in a tense attitude, listening, precisely as Biggles had done a few minutes before. Then, still without making a sound, he glided forward into the room.

For one ghastly moment Biggles thought he was coming straight to the wardrobe, and he had already braced himself for the shock of meeting when the man stepped aside and disappeared from his limited line of vision. For a moment he wondered if he had gone to the electric light switch with the object of turning it on, but the half-expected click did not come. Nor did the man reappear. Nothing happened. All was as silent as the grave. A minute passed, and another, and still nothing happened.

Then began a period of time which to Biggles' keyed-up nerves seemed like eternity; but still nothing happened. Where was the man? What was he doing? Was he still in the room? Could it be possible that he had slipped out of the window again without being noticed? No, that was quite impossible. Had he in some way opened the door and gone out into the corridor? Definitely no; in such an aching silence, for any one to attempt to turn the handle, much less the lock, without being heard, was manifestly absurd. What, then, was happening?

Such were Biggles' thoughts as he stood in his stuffy hiding-place fighting to steady his palpitating heart. Another ten minutes passed slowly and he began to wonder if there had been a man at all. Could the whole thing have been a vision conjured up by his already overtaxed nerves? The tension became electric in its intensity, and he knew he could not stand the strain much longer. Could he rush to the window, throw himself through, and bolt before the man in the room had recovered from the shock of discovering that he was not alone? He thought he could, but it was a desperate expedient that he preferred not to undertake until it became vitally necessary.

Then at last the silence was broken, broken by a sound which, as it reached his ears, seemed to turn his blood to ice. He had heard it many times before, and it never failed to fill him with a vague dread, but in his present position it literally paralysed him. It was the slow dragging gait of a lame man, and it was coming down the corridor. Then it stopped and there was a faint tap, tap, and Biggles knew that von Stalhein was propping his stick against the wall while he felt for his keys. In his agitated imagination he could see him, follow his every action, and the grinding of the key in the lock sounded like the first laborious move of a piece of badly oiled machinery. Slowly the door creaked open on its hinges. There was a sharp click, a blaze of blinding light, and von Stalhein stepped into the room.

At that moment the Arab sprang. Biggles saw him streak across the room with a brown arm upraised, and caught the flash of steel. But if the Arab hoped to catch the German unaware, he was doomed to disappointment.

Never in his life before had Biggles seen anything quite so swift as that which followed. With a lithe movement that would have been miraculous even for an athlete, von Stalhein dived forward with a galvanic jerk; the top part of his body twisted, and the curved blade that was aimed at his throat missed his shoulder by what must have been literally a hair's breadth. His sticks crashed to the floor. All the force of the Arab's arm must have been behind the blow, for his lunge carried him beyond the German, who was round in a flash. His hand darted to his hip pocket, but before he could draw the weapon he obviously kept there the

Arab was on him again, and he was compelled to use both hands to fight off his attack.

Again the Arab sprang, and as his right arm flashed down von Stalhein caught it with his left, while his right groped through the folds of his flowing burnous for the brown throat. In that position they remained while Biggles could have counted ten, looking for all the world like a piece of magnificent statuary. Neither of them spoke; only the swift intake of breath revealed the quivering energy that was being expended by each of them to hold the other off. Then the tableau snapped into lightning-like activity.

Biggles couldn't see just what happened. All he knew was that the knife crashed to the floor; at the same moment the Arab tore himself free and flung himself at the window. He went through it like a greyhound, but, even so, the German was faster. His right hand flashed down and came up gripping a squat automatic, and at the precise moment that the Arab disappeared from sight a spurt of yellow flame streaked across the room. Von Stalhein was at the window before the crash of the report had died away; with the agility of an eel he threw his legs across the sill and sprang downward out of sight.

Biggles seized his opportunity; he stepped out of the wardrobe, closed it behind him, darted to the door and sped down the corridor. He hesitated as he reached the main entrance, eyes seeking the sentry, but no one was in sight, so he ran out and took refuge behind the nearest hangar. At that stage he would have asked nothing more than to be allowed to return to his room, but he saw figures hurrying towards the fort from the Mess, so he turned about and ran back as if he had heard the report of the shot and was anxious to know the cause. Doors were banging inside and voices were

163

calling; he paid no attention to them but ran round the side of the building, and then pulled up with a jerk as he almost collided with von Stalhein and the door sentry, who were bending over a recumbent figure on the ground. He saw that it was the Arab.

'Good gracious, von Stalhein,' he exclaimed, 'what's happened? What was that shot?'

'Nothing very much,' replied the German coolly. 'Fellow tried to knife me, that's all. One of the sheikhs who was on the raid the other night; the poor fools are blaming me because the thing went wrong. By the way, where have you just sprung from?'

It was on the tip of Biggles' tongue to say 'from my room', but something warned him to be careful. Instead, 'I was admiring the night from the tarmac,' he smiled; 'I can't sit indoors this weather. Why?'

'Because I looked into your room just now to have a word with you, and you weren't there,' was the casual reply.

Biggles caught his breath as he realized how nearly he had made a blunder. 'What did you want me for?' he inquired.

'Oh, merely a job the Count had in mind, but don't worry about it now; I'll see you in the morning. I shall have to stay and see this mess cleared up, confound it.' Von Stalhein touched the Arab with the toe of his patent leather shoe.

'All right. Then I think I'll get to bed,' returned Biggles, as several officers and mechanics joined the party.

Safely out of sight round the corner of a hangar he mopped his face with a handkerchief. 'My gosh,' he muttered, 'this business is nothing but one shock after another. "Where have you just sprung from?" he asked. I felt like saying, "And where the dickens have *you* come from?'' He couldn't have been in that machine that took off, after all; I'm beginning to take too much for granted, which doesn't pay, evidently, at this game. And so he's got a job for me in the morning, eh? Well, with any luck I shan't be taking on many more jobs in this part of the world, I hope.'

Chapter 16
Checked

The next morning he was awakened by his batman*
bringing early morning tea. He got out of bed, lit a
cigarette, and sat by the open window while he con-
sidered the results of his investigations. How far had
he progressed? How much had he learned about El
Shereef, the German super-spy? Had he arrived at a
stage when, figuratively speaking, he could lay his cards
on Major Raymond's desk and ask to be posted back
to his old squadron, leaving the Intelligence people to
do the rest? No, he decided regretfully, he had not. He
had learned something, enough perhaps to end von
Stalhein's activities, but that was not enough, for while
the British Intelligence Staff might agree that he had
concluded his task, something inside told him that it
was still incomplete; that something more, the unmask-
ing of a deeper plot than either he or British headquarters at first suspected, remained to be done. Just
what that was he did not know, but he had a vague
suspicion, and at the moment he felt he was standing
on the threshold of discoveries that might alter the
whole course of the war in that part of the world.
Moreover, it was unlikely that another British agent
would ever again be in such a sound position to bring
about the exposure; so it was up to him to hang on
whatever the cost to himself.

* An attendant serving an officer. A position discontinued in today's
Royal Air Force.

That von Stalhein was the super-spy, El Shereef, he no longer doubted, for it was hardly possible that there could be two German spies masquerading as Arabs behind the British lines, and that von Stalhein did adopt Arab disguise was certain; the incident at the oasis was sufficient proof of that. If further proof were needed there was the business of the feigned limp, which he felt was all part of a clever pose to throw possible investigators off the scent. The limp was so pronounced, and he played the part of a lame man to such perfection, that the very act of abandoning it would have been a disguise in itself. No one could even think of von Stalhein without the infirmity. For what purpose other than espionage, or disguise, should he pretend to be incapacitated when he was not?

He knew now that von Stalhein was as active as any normal man. The way he had behaved when attacked by the Arab in his room revealed that, for he had dropped his sticks and dashed to the window with a speed that would have done credit to a professional runner. If he were not El Shereef, why the pose? As Erich von Stalhein he made his headquarters at Zabala; at night he changed, and under the pseudonym of El Shereef, worked behind the British lines, coming and going by means of a special detailed aeroplane. And the more Biggles thought about it the more he was convinced that he was right.

'The pilot flies him over, lands him well behind the lines—at the oasis for instance—and then comes home. Later, at a pre-arranged time and place, he goes over and picks him up,' he mused. 'That's what Mayer was doing the day he picked me up. Mayer landed for von Stalhein, but when he found me there instead he knew he had to bring me back. If only I could catch von Stalhein in the act of landing, there would be an end to it, but I'll bet he never again uses the place where *I* was picked up; he'd be too cunning for that; he doesn't trust me a yard, in spite of the fact that he has no foundation for his suspicions. He must have an instinct for danger like a cat. The only other way to nab him would be to find out the Arab name he adopts when he is over there, hanging about our troops picking up information. The thing I can't get over is that shadow on the tent, and but for the fact that he must have been somewhere around in order to learn that I was a prisoner, and then effect my rescue, I should feel inclined to think that I'd been mistaken. It's rather funny he has never mentioned a thing to me, taken credit for getting me out of the mess. No, perhaps it isn't funny. Oh, dash it, I don't know . . . unless . . .'

He stared thoughtfully at the desert for some time, drumming on the window-sill with his fingers. 'Well, I'd better go and see what the Count wants, I suppose,' he concluded, as he finished his toilet and went down to the Mess to breakfast, after which he walked along to the fort. He found von Stalhein in the headquarters office, but the Count had not yet arrived.

'Good morning, Brunow,' greeted the German affably. 'Quite a good photo—look.' He passed the last photograph Biggles had taken of Mayer's burning Halberstadt.

'Good morning, von Stalhein,' replied Biggles, taking it and looking at it closely, aware that that the German's eyes were on him. He finished his scrutiny and passed it back, wondering if von Stalhein had over-looked something in the photograph which he had spotted instantly. The photograph had been taken from a very low altitude and from an oblique angle, which showed not only the charred, smoking wreck but the desert beyond. Across the soft sand where he had landed ran a line of wheel tracks; they began some distance from the crash and ran off the top right-hand corner of the photograph. He looked up to see von Stalhein looking at him; his eyes were smiling mockingly, but there was no smile about his thin lips.

'I may be mistaken, but I understood you to say that you didn't land,' observed the German, in a low careless voice that nevertheless held a hard, steely quality.

Biggles raised his eyebrows. 'No, you were not mistaken,' he replied; 'why did you say that?'

'I was wondering how the wheel marks got there, that's all.'

Biggles laughed. 'Oh, those,' he said. 'Those were the marks made by my home-made trailer, I expect—have a cigarette?'

He offered his case as if his explanation of such a trivial point was sufficient—as indeed it was.

'Of course,' said von Stalhein, slowly—very slowly. 'Funny, I didn't think of that.'

'One cannot always expect to think of everything,' rejoined Biggles simply. 'What does the Count want—do you know?'

'Here he is, so he'll tell you himself,' answered von Stalhein shortly.

Biggles sprang to attention. 'Good morning, sir,' he said.

'Good morning, Brunow— morning, Erich. Going to be hot again,' observed the Count, dropping into his chair behind the desk. And then, glancing up at Biggles, he asked, 'Has Hauptmann von Stalhein told you what we were discussing last night?'

'No, sir.'

'I see.' The Count unfastened his stiff upright collar. 'Well, the position is this,' he went on. 'As you are no doubt aware, the chief reason why you were sent here was because of your knowledge of the English and their language. It was thought that you might be able to undertake duties that would be impossible for a—one of our own people. You have a British R.F.C. uniform, and we have British aeroplanes, yet neither have been fully exploited. In fact, you are rapidly becoming an ordinary flying officer engaged on routine duties, and in that capacity you have done remarkably well; in fact, if it goes on one of the *Staffels* will be putting in a request for you to be posted to them. I think it's time we did something about it, don't you?'

'As you wish, sir. I have thought about it myself, but I didn't mention it because I thought you'd give me orders for special duty when you were ready.'

'Quite so.' The Count turned to von Stalhein. 'We shall make a good German officer of him yet, Erich,' he observed dryly, in German.

'Thank you, sir,' put in Biggles absent-mindedly, in the same language.

'Ah-ha, so you are progressing with your German, too,' asserted the Count, raising his eyebrows.

Biggles flushed slightly, for the words had slipped out unthinkingly. 'I'm doing my best, and what with my book and conversations in the Mess, I am picking it up slowly,' he explained.

'Capital. But let us come to this business we are here for,' continued the Count. He lit a long black cigar and studied the glowing end closely before he went on. 'Last night I was merely concerned with the idea of sending you over to the British lines for a day or two to pick up any odd scraps of information that might be useful, paying particular regard to the preparations the British are making for the attack we know is soon to be launched near Gaza—at least, everything points to the battle being fought there. Since then, however, a blow has fallen the importance of which cannot be exaggerated. It is, in fact, the most serious set-back we have had for a long time. Fortunately it does not affect us personally, but I hear that General Headquarters in Jerusalem is in a fever about it; if we could recover what we have lost, it would be a feather in our caps.'

'In your cap, you mean,' thought Biggles, but he said nothing.

'Tell me, Brunow'—the Count dropped his voice to little more than a whisper—'have you ever heard of one who is called El Shereef?'

Had he pulled out a revolver and fired point blank he could hardly have given Biggles a bigger shock. How he kept his face immobile he never knew, for the words set every nerve in his body jangling. He pretended to think for a moment before he replied. 'I seem to recall it, sir, but in what connexion I cannot think— yes, I have it. You remember the first day I came here I landed at Kantara. I heard some of the officers in the Mess using the name quite a lot, but I didn't pay much attention to it.'

'Then I will tell you. El Shereef was a—an agent, a German agent. Not only was he the cleverest agent in Palestine, but in the world.'

'Was . . . ?'

'He has been caught at last.'

Biggles felt the room rocking about him, but he continued staring straight at the Count, struggling to prevent his face from betraying what he was thinking. 'What a pity,' he said at last. For the life of him he couldn't think of anything else to say.

'Pity! it's a tragedy—an overwhelming misfortune. He was taken yesterday in a cunningly set trap by Major Sterne, who as you may know is one of the cleverest men on the British side.'

'By Major Sterne,' repeated Biggles foolishly.

The Count nodded. 'So we understand. The British have made no announcement about it—nor do we expect them to—yet. But General Headquarters, by means known only to themselves, got the news through late last night.'

Von Stalhein was lighting a fresh cigarette as if the matter hardly interested him.

Biggles tried to think, but could not. His mind seemed to have collapsed in complete chaos as all his so-called facts, conjectures, and suppositions crashed to the ground. He could hardly follow what the Count was saying when he continued.

'Well, there it is. The British will give him a trial—of sorts—of course, but we shall know only one thing more for certain—and that soon—and that is that El Shereef has faced a firing party. If you are to do anything it will have to be done at once.'

'Do anything, sir,' ejaculated Biggles. 'Me! What can I do?'

'You can get into the British lines. I was hoping that you might try to effect a rescue.'

Biggles nearly laughed aloud, for he felt that he was going insane. Was the Count seriously asking him to rescue El Shereef, when . . . ? The thing was too utterly ridiculous. He saw the Count was waiting for his answer. 'I'll do anything I can, sir,' he offered. 'If you could give me any further information that might be useful I should be grateful.'

The Count shook his head. 'All I can tell you is that El Shereef will probably be sent under special escort to British General Headquarters for interrogation.'

'Then I'd better go over and do what I can,' said Biggles thoughtfully; and then added in a flash of inspiration, 'Can you give me any idea of what he looks

172

like, so that I shall be able to recognize him when I see him?'

'Yes, I can do that,' agreed the Count. 'He is, as you no doubt imagine, really a German, although he will of course be dressed as an Arab. He has lived with the Arabs for so long that he is nearly one of them—looks Arab—thinks Arab—speaks Arabic. Tall, brown—really brown, not merely grease paint—drooping black moustache. Dark eyes, and rather a big nose, like the beak of a hawk. Not much of a description, but it's the best I can give you. If you can get near him, show your ring and he'll understand. He will still have his hidden about him if the British didn't take it away when they searched him.'

'Very good, sir; I'll get off right away.' Biggles did not so much as glance at von Stalhein as he saluted, turned on his heel and departed to his room.

When he reached it he slumped down wearily on his bed and gave expression to his disappointment and mortification, for his feelings at that moment were not unlike those of a very tired man who, in the act of sitting down, realizes that some one has pulled the chair away from under him. After a period of deadly risk and anxiety he thought he had the situation well summed up, and all he needed to do to win was to play his trump cards carefully. The knowledge that his cards were useless was a disappointment not easily overcome, and it was followed by an almost overwhelming sense of depression, for if what the Count had told him was true, he had been running on a false scent all along. The only redeeming thing about the new development was that, if the British had really caught El Shereef, then this work was finished, and there was no longer any reason why he should stay at Zabala. Officially, his retirement from the scene would now be permissible, even though he had failed, but he knew he could not conscientiously do so while in his heart he was still certain that von Stalhein was engaged in some sinister scheme about which the British authorities knew nothing. Suppose the story were not true? Suppose the whole thing was pure fabrication, a story invented by the Count and von Stalhein to draw a red herring across the trail of British agents whom they suspected — or knew — to be engaged in counter-espionage behind their lines. Conversely, might it not be a gigantic piece of bluff devised by the British Intelligence Staff to mislead the Germans, or cause them to make a move which might betray the very man whom they claimed to have caught? Both theories were possible.

Thinking the new situation over, Biggles felt like a man who, faced with the task of unravelling a tangled ball of string, sees a dozen ends sticking out, but does not know which is the right one. 'I've had a few boneshakers since I started this job, but this one certainly is a bazouka,' he mused. 'Well, I suppose I'd better do something about it, and the best thing I can do is to push off through the atmosphere to Kantara to find out how much truth there is in it.'

He changed into his R.F.C. uniform, pulled his overalls on over it, went down to the tarmac, ordered out the Bristol Fighter, and landed at Kantara exactly thirty-five minutes later. He taxied up to the hangars, and telling the duty N.C.O. to leave his machine where it was in case he needed it urgently, went straight to Major Raymond's tent.

He found the Major working at his desk.

'Good morning, Bigglesworth —'

But Biggles was too impatient to indulge in conventional greetings. 'Is this tale true about your catching El Shereef, sir,' he asked abruptly.

'Quite true.'

Biggles stared. 'Well, I'll be shot for the son of a gun,' he muttered. 'You're quite sure—I mean, you're not just spinning a yarn?'

'Good gracious, no. But how did you know about it?'

'Von Faubourg told me this morning.'

'He wasn't long getting the news then.'

'So it seems. How did you work it?'

'Sterne did it. He's been on the trail for some time, working in his own way. He managed to pick up a clue and laid a pretty trap, and El Shereef, cunning as he is, walked straight into it.'

'That's what the Huns told me,' nodded Biggles. 'It begins to look as if it's true.'

'Of course it's true—we've got him here.'

'What! at Kantara?'

'Well, at Jebel Zaloud, the village just behind. General Headquarters are there. They've had El Shereef there trying to get some information out of him, but it's no use. He won't speak. He won't do anything else if it comes to that—won't eat or drink. He's an Arab, you know.'

'Arab? You mean he's disguised as an Arab?'

'If it's a disguise, then it's a thundering good one.'

'It would be. He's lived amongst the Arabs half his life, until he is one, or as near as makes no difference. The Count told me so himself.'

'I don't know about that, but it's no wonder things went wrong over here. He is—or rather, was—one of our most trusted Sheikhs. He's a fellow with a big following, too.'

'How do you know it's El Shereef?'

'Sterne was sure of it before he collared him. When we took him he was wearing one of those same rings that you've got—the German Secret Service ring. I've got it here: here it is. He had also got some very interesting documents on him—plans of British positions, and so on.'

Biggles picked up the ring that the Major had tossed on to the table and looked at it with interest. 'I should like to see this cove,' he said quietly.

'I think it could be arranged, although I can't see much point in it. You'll have to make haste, though.'

'Why?'

'He was tried by a specially convened Field General Court Martial this morning and sentenced to death.'

'Good God! When is sentence to be carried out?'

'To-day, some time. He's too tricky a customer to keep hanging about. He'll certainly be shot before sundown.'

Biggles jaw set grimly. 'That's awkward,' he said.

'Why?'

'Because I've been sent over here to rescue him.'

It was the Major's turn to look startled. 'Are you serious?' he asked incredulously.

'Too true I am.'

'What are you going to do about it?'

'Nothing—now. I'm through. If you've got the fellow, then that's the end of the story as far as I'm concerned.'

'That's what I thought; in fact, that's why I sent Lacey over to let you know.'

'You did what?'

'Sent Lacey over. I couldn't do less. There was no point in your going on risking your neck at Zabala.'

'Where's Algy now?'

'He's gone. He took off just before you landed. He's going to do the message-dropping stunt in the olive grove. It's a pity he went, but naturally I didn't expect the Huns would tell you about our catching El Shereef.'

Biggles nodded sagely. 'Which, to my mind, is a perfectly good reason why you might have guessed they'd do it,' he declared. 'In my experience, it's the very last thing that you'd expect that always happens at this game. My word! dog-fighting* is child's play to it.'

'Well, what are you going to do? I'm busy over this affair, as you may imagine.'

'Just as a matter of curiosity I'd like to have a dekko at this nimble chap who is called El Shereef.'

'Very well; after what you've done we can hardly refuse such a natural request. I'll see if it can be arranged.' The Major reached for his telephone.

---

* An aerial battle rather than a hit and run attack.

Chapter 17
Hare and Hounds

Two hours later Biggles again sat in Major Raymond's tent with his face buried in his hands; the Major was busy writing on a pad. 'How's this?' he said, passing two sheets of paper. 'The first is an official notification of the execution that will appear in to-night's confidential orders; the other is the notice that will be issued to the press. Naturally, we make as much of a thing like this as we can; it's good propaganda, and it bucks up the public at home to know that we are as quick-witted as the Huns.'

Biggles read the notices. 'They seem to be O.K., sir,' he said, passing them back. 'I'll be going now,' he added, rising and picking up his cap.

'You still insist in going back to Zabala?'

'I don't want to go, sir, don't think that, but I think it's up to me to try to get the truth about von Stalhein's game while I can come and go. I know I said I wouldn't go back, but I've been thinking it over. I shan't be long, anyway. If I find things are getting too hot I'll pack up and report here.'

'As you wish,' agreed the Major.

Biggles walked towards the door. 'Cheerio for the present, then, sir,' he said. 'You might remember me to Algy when he comes back.'

'He's probably back by now; can't you stay and have a word with him?'

'No, I haven't time now; besides, I've nothing particular to talk about,' decided Biggles. Lost in thought, he walked slowly back to where he had left his Bristol, climbed into the cockpit, and took off. Still in a brown study, he hardly bothered to watch the sky, for while he was over the British side of the lines he had nothing to fear, and over the German side the white bar on his wings made him safe from attack from German aeroplanes.

Once he caught sight of a large formation of Pfalz Scouts, but he paid no attention to them; he did not even watch them but continued on a straight course for Zabala, still turning over in his mind the knotty problems that beset him.

It was, therefore, with a start of surprise and annoyance that he was aroused from his reverie by the distant clatter of a machine-gun, and while he was in the act of looking back for the source of the noise he was galvanized into activity by a staccato burst which he knew from experience was well inside effective range. Cursing himself for his carelessness, he half-rolled desperately, but not before he had felt the vicious thud of bullets ripping through his machine. 'What the dickens do the fools think they're playing at?' he snarled, as he levelled out and saw that he was in the middle of a swarm of Pfalz. 'They must be blind,' he went on furiously, as he threw the Bristol into a steep bank in order to display the white bar on his top plane. But either the Germans did not see it or they deliberately ignored it, for two or three of them darted in, guns going, obviously with the intention of shooting him down.

Biggles knew that something had gone wrong, but the present was no time to wonder what it was. He must act quickly if he was to escape the fate that he had often meted out to others, but he was at once faced with a difficult problem. At the back of his mind still lingered the conviction that the Pfalz pilots had forgotten all about his distinguishing mark, and would presently see and remember it, but whether that was so or not, the only thing that really counted at the moment was that they were doing their best to kill him. And by reason of their numbers they were likely to succeed. In the ordinary way, had he been flying a real British machine, the matter would not have worried him unduly; he would simply have fought the best fight he could as long as his machine held together and remained in the air. He had, in fact, fought against even greater odds and escaped, but then he had been able to give as good as he got. 'If I shoot any of these fellows down it puts the tin hat on my ever going back to Zabala, even if I do get away with it,' he thought desperately, as he turned round and round, kicking on right and left rudder alternately to avoid the streams of lead that were being poured at him from all directions.

He knew that the only thing he could do was to attempt to escape, either by trying to get back to the British lines, or by making a dash for Zabala, which was nearer. He would have spun down and landed had it been possible to land, but it was not, for the country below was a vast tract of broken rock and camel-thorn bushes. Nevertheless, he threw the Bristol into a spin with the object of getting as near to the ground as possible, and 'hedge-hopping'—or rather, rock-hopping—home. Looking back over his shoulder he saw the Pfalz spinning down behind him. He pulled out at a hundred feet above the ground, but still eased the stick forward until his wheels were literally skimming the rocks; and swerving from side to side to throw the gunners off their mark, raced for Zabala. Behind him screamed the Pfalz, like a pack of hounds after the hare.

Occasionally the sound of guns reached his ears, and once in a while a bullet bit into the machine, but the chance of being hit by a stray shot was the risk he had to take. By flying low he had made shooting difficult for the Boche pilots, who dare not dive as steeply as they would have liked to have done, and could have done higher up. Their difficulty was that of a diver who knows that the water into which he is about to plunge is shallow; to dive deep would mean hitting the bottom. In the case of the Pfalz, they dare not risk over shooting* their target for fear of crashing into the ground. So, unable to dive, they could only hang behind and take long shots. Their task was not made any easier by the fact that the Bristol did not fly on the same course for more than two or three seconds at a time; it turned and twisted from side to side like a snipe when it hears the sportsmen's guns.

This sort of flying needs a cool head and steady nerves, and Biggles possessed both; his many battles in France had given him those desirable qualities. He had to have eyes in the back of his head, as the saying goes, for it was necessary to keep a sharp look-out in front for possible obstacles, and at the same time keep watch behind for the more daring pilots who sometimes took a chance and came in close, whereupon he would turn at right angles and dash off on a new course, thereby upsetting their aim.

In spite of his precarious position, he smiled as the chase roared over the heads of a squadron of cavalry, sending the horses stampeding in all directions. On another occasion a German Staff car that was racing along the road down which he was then roaring in the opposite direction, pulled up so quickly that he was

* To fly past another aeroplane when following through an attack.

given the never-to-be-forgotten spectacle of a German general in full uniform, with his head through the windscreen.

As he approached Zabala the German scouts doubled their efforts to stop him, evidently under the impression that the British two-seater intended to bomb their aerodrome, and the consequence was that Biggles, who by this time was not in the least particular as to how or where he got down, made a landing that was as spectacular as it was unusual. He throttled back, side-slipped off his last few feet of height, flattened out and hurtled down-wind across the sun-baked sandy aerodrome. His wheels touched, but he did not stop. The hangars seemed to rush towards him, and he braced himself for the collision that seemed inevitable.

Leaning over the side of his cockpit to get a clear view round his windscreen, he saw German mechanics hauling a Halberstadt out of his path with frantic haste; others were unashamedly sprinting for cover. But the machine was beginning to lose speed, and fifty yards from the tarmac Biggles risked applying a little rudder and aileron, although he clenched his teeth as he did so, fully expecting to hear the undercarriage collapse under the strain. A grinding jar proclaimed the Bristol's protest, but the wheels stood up to the terrific strain, and slowly the machine swung round until it was tearing straight along the tarmac in a cloud of dust.

The Count himself, and von Stalhein, who had heard the shouting and had dashed out to see what was happening, just had time to throw themselves aside as the Bristol ran to a standstill in front of the fort, leaving a line of staring mechanics and swirling sand to mark it tempestuous course.

'What the devil do you think you're doing?' roared the Count, white with anger.

Biggles climbed out and pushed up his goggles before he replied. 'With all respect to you, sir,' he said bitterly, 'I think that is a question that might well be put to the pilots of the Pfalz *Staffel*.'

'What do you mean?' asked the Count, glancing up at the scouts, some of which were already landing, while others circled round awaiting their turn.

Biggles glared at von Stalhein as a new suspicion flashed into his mind. 'They've done their best to shoot me down, sir,' he told the Count. 'Look at my machine,' he added, nearly choking with rage as he thought he saw the solution of the whole thing. Von Stalhein still mistrusted him, and had deliberately set the Pfalz on to him as the easiest way to removing him without awkward questions or the formality of a court martial.

The Count looked in surprise at the bullet holes in the wings and tail of the Bristol. 'I don't understand this,' he said with a puzzled expression. 'Do you, Erich?' He turned to von Stalhein, who shook his head.

'I suppose there must be an explanation,' he said calmly. 'Here come the Pfalz pilots: perhaps they can tell us what it is.'

The scout pilots who now arrived on the scene pulled up short when they saw the pilot of the Bristol Fighter; they seemed to have difficulty in finding words. For a few moments nobody spoke. The Count looked from one to the other. Von Stalhein waited, with a faint inscrutable smile on his face. Biggles glared at all of them in turn. 'Well, he said at last, 'what about it?'

One of the German pilots said something quickly and half apologetically to the Count; Biggles caught the words, 'mark and wings'.

Von Faubourg started and turned to Biggles. 'He says you've no markings on your wings,' he cried.

'No markings,' exclaimed Biggles incredulously.

'Impossible!' He swung up and stood on the side of the fuselage from where he could see the whole of the top plane. From end to end it was painted the standard dull biscuit colour; there was not a speck of white on it anywhere. He stared as if it were some strange new creature that he had never seen before, while his brain struggled to absorb this miracle, for it seemed no less. He jumped down, eyes seeking the maker's number on the tail; and then he understood. It was not the number of his original machine. For some reason as incomprehensible as it was unbelievable, the machine he had flown over to Kantara that morning had been removed while it was standing on the tarmac, and another substituted in its place. It must have been done during the three hours he was with Major Raymond or away from the aerodrome.

He pulled himself together with an effort and turned to the Count. 'He's quite right, sir,' he said, 'there is no white mark. But do not ask me to explain it, because I cannot. The only suggestion that I can offer is that a change of machines took place while I was at Kantara.'

The Count was obviously unconvinced, but as he could offer no better explanation he dismissed the matter with a wave of his hand. 'Come along to my office, Brunow, I want you,' he said, and with von Stalhein at his side, disappeared into the porch of the fort.

Biggles turned to follow, but before he went in he turned to one of the Pfalz pilots who he knew spoke a little English and said, 'How was it you happened to be where you were—when I came along?'

'Well, we are usually somewhere about there,' replied the German, 'but as we were taking off von Stalhein told us that we should probably find some British machines there this morning.'

'I see,' said Biggles, 'thanks.' Then he followed the Count into his office.

'What happened over the other side?' was the curt question that greeted him as he stepped into the room.

'I'm sorry, sir, but I was too late to do anything,' answered Biggles simply.

'Too late?'

'Sheikh Haroun Ibn Said, better known as El Shereef, of the German Intelligence Staff, was tried by Field General Court Martial this morning and sentenced to death for espionage,' said Biggles in a low voice. 'The sentence was carried out within an hour on the grounds of the undesirability of keeping such a dangerous man in captivity. I'm not sure, but I believe the British are making an official announcement about it to-night.'

The Count sat down slowly in his chair and looked at von Stalhein. Biggles also looked at him, and thought he detected a faint gleam of triumph in the unflinching eyes. There was silence for a few minutes broken only by the Count tapping on his teeth with a lead pencil. 'Ah, well,' he said at last with a shrug of his massive shoulders, 'we have failed, but we did our best. Did you learn anything else while you were over there?'

'Only that there seems to be a good deal of activity going on, sir.'

'We are already aware of that. Anything else?'

'No, sir.'

'What excuse did you give to account for your presence at Kantara?'

'The same as before. I said I was a delivery pilot; they are always coming and going and nobody questioned it.'

'I see. That's all for the present.'

Biggles saluted and marched out of the room into

185

the blazing sunshine, but he did not go straight to his room, which, as events showed, was a fortunate thing. Instead, he walked along to the hangar where the two British machines were kept, with the object of testing a theory he had formed during his interview with the Count. Several mechanics were at work on the damaged Bristol, covering the bullet holes with small slips of fabric, but he went past them to where the Pup was standing in a corner and put his hand on the engine. One touch told him all he needed to know. The engine was still warm.

'I'm right,' he thought. 'That's how it was done.'

Chapter 18
An Unwelcome Visitor

'Yes, that's how he did it, the cunning beggar,' he mused again, as he walked back slowly to his room and changed into his German uniform. 'One false move now, and he'll be on me like a ton of—hello! what's going on over there, I wonder?' He broke off his soliloquy to watch with casual interest a little scene that was being enacted at the entrance gate of the camp, which was quite close to his quarters, and which he could just see by leaning out of the window. The sound of what seemed to be an argument reached him, and looking out to see what it was all about, he noticed that a service tender had drawn up to discharge a single passenger who was now engaged in a heated discussion with the N.C.O. in charge of the guard.

From his actions it was clear that he was trying to obtain admission to the station, but he was in civilian clothes, and the attitude of the N.C.O. suggested that he was not satisfied with his credentials. The man's suitcase had been stood on the ground, and as Biggles automatically read the name that was painted on its side in black letters he drew in his breath sharply, while his fingers gripped the window-sill until his knuckles showed white through the tan. The name on the suitcase was L. Brunow.

For a moment he came near to panic, and it was all he could do to prevent himself from dashing down to the tarmac, jumping into the first aeroplane he came to, and placing himself behind the British lines in the

187

shortest possible space of time. He knew that he was in the tightest corner of his life, but he did not lose his head. He slipped his German Mauser revolver into his pocket and hurried round to the gate.

'What is the matter?' he asked the N.C.O. in German—one of the phrases he had learnt by heart.

The N.C.O. saluted and said something too quickly for him to catch, so Biggles resorted to the friend that had so often before helped him in difficult situations— bluff. He waved the N.C.O. aside, and indicated by his manner that the newcomer was known to him, and that he would accept responsibility for him. At the same time he picked up the suitcase and held it close to his side so that the name could not be read.

The real Brunow—for Biggles was in no doubt whatever as to the identity of the new arrival—wiped the perspiration from his face with a handkerchief. 'Can you speak English by any chance?' he said apologetically; 'I'm afraid my German isn't very good.'

'A leedle,' replied Biggles awkwardly. 'I understand better than I speak perhaps—yes?'

'Thank goodness. Then will you show me Count von Faubourg's office; I have an important message for him.'

'Yes, I will show you,' replied Biggles, but the thought that flashed through his mind was, 'Yes, I'll bet you have'. 'Der Count has just gone away,' he went on aloud. 'You must have the thirst, after your journey in der sun. I go to my room for a drink now—perhaps you come—no?'

'Thanks, I will,' replied Brunow with alacrity. 'I can't stand this heat.'

'It vas derrible,' agreed Biggles, as he led the way to his room, wondering what he was going to do with the man when he got there.

Brunow threw himself into a chair while Biggles took from the cupboard two glasses, a siphon of soda-water, and a bottle of brandy that he kept for visitors. The amount of brandy that he poured into Brunow's glass nearly made him blush, but Brunow did not seem to notice it, so he added a little soda-water and passed it over. His own glass he filled from the siphon, at the same time regretfully observing that he had had a touch of dysentery, and was forbidden alcohol by doctor's orders. He half smiled as Brunow drank deeply like a thirsty man—as he probably was—and decided in his mind that whatever happened Brunow must not be allowed to leave the room, for if ever he reached the Count's office his own hours were numbered.

'How long is the Count going to be, do you think?' inquired Brunow, setting down his empty glass, which Biggles casually refilled.

'He may be gone some time,' he answered in his best pseudo-German accent. 'Why, is it something important—yes?'

Brunow took another drink. 'I should say it is,' he retorted, settling himself down more comfortably in the chair. 'Too important to be put in a dispatch,' he added, rather boastfully, as an afterthought.

Biggles whistled softly, and made up his mind that his best chance of getting into the man's confidence was through his vanity. 'So! and they send you,' he exclaimed.

'That's right,' declared Brunow. 'They've sent me all the way from Berlin rather than trust the telegraph or the post-bag.' He leaned forward confidentially and looked up into Biggles' face. 'Perhaps I shouldn't tell you—keep this to yourself—but there's going to be a fine old row when I see the Count.'

Biggles laughed and refilled the glasses. 'That will

be not new,' he said. 'We of the staff have plenty of those.'

'But this one will be something to remember,' Brunow told him with a leer.

Biggles looked sceptical, which seemed to annoy Brunow.

'What would you say if I told you there was a spy here—here—here at Zabala?' he asked bellicosely.

Biggles shrugged his shoulders. 'It would be a funny place where there were no rumours about spies,' he said inconsequentially.

The combined effects of the heat and the brandy were becoming apparent in Brunow's manner. He put his feet up on the table and frowned at Biggles through half-closed eyes. 'Are you suggesting that I don't know what I'm talking about?' he inquired coldly. 'You'll be telling me next that I'm drunk,' he added with the aggressive indignation of a man who is well on his way to intoxication.

'I should hope not,' replied Biggles, in well simulated surprise. 'We are all two-bottle men here. Have another drink?' Without waiting for a reply, he filled the glasses again, inwardly disgusted that a man on special duty could behave in a manner so utterly foolish and irresponsible. 'Well,' he thought, 'it's either him or me for it, so it's no time to be squeamish.'

'Funny thing, you know,' went on Brunow confidingly; 'I'm not really German, but I went to Germany to offer my services. When I got there and told them my name, what do you think they did?'

'I'm no good at riddles,' admitted Biggles.

'They threw me in clink,' declared the other, picking up his glass.

'Clink?'

'In quod—you know, prison.

190

'*Donner blitz**,' muttered Biggles, looking shocked.

'They did,' went on Brunow reflectively, sinking a little lower in his chair. 'Had the brass face to tell me that I was already serving in the Secret Service. What would you say if any one told you that, eh?'

'Biggles shook his head. 'Impossible!' he exclaimed, for want of something better to say.

'That's what I told them,' swore Brunow, waxing eloquent. 'The funny thing is, though, they were right. Can you beat that, eh?'

'It vas not possible.'

'Wasn't it! Ha! that's all that you know about it. I kicked up a proper stink and showed them my papers; when they saw those they smelt a rat and got busy. Quick wasn't the word. To make a long story short, they found that some skunk had got in under the canvas and was pretending to be me—*me*! What do you know about that?'

Biggles knew quite a lot about it but he did not say so. 'Too bad,' he murmured sympathetically.

'Too bad!' exploded Brunow, starting up. 'Is that all you've got to say about it? Don't you realize that this other fellow is a *spy*? Well, I've got it in for him,' he declared venomously, as he sank back. 'They believe it's a fellow named Bigglesworth, who's disappeared from France, though it beats me how they found that out. But whoever he is, he's here at Zabala.'

Biggles poured out more brandy with a hand that shook slightly, for Brunow had raised his voice. Twilight was falling over the desert, and in the hush the sound of voices carried far.

'So you've come here to put an end to his little game,

---

* By thunder!

eh?' he said quietly. 'Good! Still, there's no need to get excited about it.'

'Who are you, telling me not to get excited about it?' fumed Brunow. 'These cursed British chucked—' He pulled up as if he realized that he was saying too much. 'I want to see them shoot this skunk Bigglesworth, and I want to see him twitch when he gets a neck full of lead. That's what I want to see,' he snarled.

'Well, maybe you will,' Biggles told him.

'That's what I've come here for. The people in Berlin were going to send a telegram; then they thought they'd send a dispatch, but in the end they decided to send a special messenger. They chose me, and here I am,' stated Brunow. 'Pretty good, eh?'

'How about another drink?' smiled Biggles, and the instant he said it he knew he had gone too far. A look of suspicion darted into Brunow's bloodshot eyes, and the corners of his mouth came down ominously. 'Say! what's the big idea?' he growled. 'Are you trying to get me tanked?'

'Tanked?' Biggles tried to look as if he did not understand.

'Yes—blotto . . . sewn up. You sit there swilling that gut-rot, lacing me with brandy, and letting me do the talking. Do you know this skate Bigglesworth? You must have met him if you're stationed here. That's it. Is he a pal of yours, or—'

Biggles could almost see Brunow's bemused brain wrestling with the problem. The half-drunken man knew he had said too much, and was trying to recall just how much he had said. Then into his eyes came suddenly a new look; it was as if a dreadful possibility had struck him. Quickly, as he stared into Biggles face, doubt changed to certainty, and with certainty came hate and fear. He sprang to his feet, and grabbing the brandy bottle by the neck, swung it upwards; the table went over with a crash. 'Curse you,' he screamed. 'You're—'

Biggles dodged the bottle that would have brained him if it had reached its mark, and grabbed him by the throat. So sudden had been the attack that he was nearly caught off his guard, but once he realized that Brunow, in a flash of drunken inspiration, had recognized him, he acted with the speed of light, knowing that at all costs he must prevent him from shouting. One call for help and he was lost.

As his right hand found Brunow's throat and choked off the cry that rose to his lips, his left hand gripped the wrist that still held the bottle and a wave of fighting fury swept over him. It was the first time in his life that he had actually made physical contact with one of the enemy, and his reaction to it was shattering in its intensity; it aroused a latent instinct to destroy that he had never suspected was in him, and the knowledge that the man was not only an enemy but a traitor fanned the red-heat of his rage to a searing white-hot flame. 'Yes,' he ground out through his clenched teeth, 'I'm Bigglesworth—you dirty traitorous rat.'

But Brunow was no weakling. He was a trifle older than Biggles, and more heavily built, but what he gained from this advantage was lost by being out of condition, although he fought with the fear of death on him.

Locked in an unyielding embrace, they lost their balance and toppled over on to the bed. For a moment they lay on it panting, and then with a sudden wrench, Brunow tore himself free; but Biggles clung to his wrist and they both crashed to the floor. The shock broke his hold and they both sprang up simultaneously.

Brunow had lost too much breath to shout; he aimed

a murderous blow with the bottle, but he was a fraction of a second too slow. Biggles sprang sideways like a cat and then darted in behind the other arm, while as he moved his right hand flashed down and up, bringing the Mauser with it. The force Brunow had put behind his blow almost over-balanced him, and before he could recover Biggles brought the butt of his gun down on the back of his head.

Brunow swayed for a moment with a look of startled surprise on his face, and then pitched forward over the table.

Biggles stood rigid, listening, wondering fearfully if the noise of the struggle had been heard, and his lips closed in a thin straight line as his worst fears were realized. Slowly dragging footsteps were coming down the corridor, accompanied by the tap, tap, of walking-sticks.

He literally flung Brunow under the bed and kicked his suitcase after him. He set the table on its legs, replaced the siphon and the bottle which had fallen from Brunow's hand, and put one of the tumblers beside it. The other had been broken and there was no time to pick up the pieces. Then he pushed the Mauser under his pillow, and flung himself down on the disarranged bed in an attitude of sleep.

With every nerve tingling, he heard the footsteps stop outside; the door was opened quietly and he knew that von Stalhein was standing looking into the room.

How long the German stood there he did not know. He did not hear him go, and for some time he dare not risk opening his eyes; but when at length he risked a peep through his lashes the door was closed again. Still, he took no chances. He got up like a man rising from a deep sleep, but seeing that the room was really empty he glided to the window and looked out. In the twilight he could just see von Stalhein limping towards the fort. 'Thought I'd been drinking, I suppose,' mused Biggles, as he began to act on the plan he had formed while lying on the bed.

Brunow must be disposed of, that was vital. How long it would be before the people in Berlin became aware of his non-arrival he did not know; nor did he care particularly. The first thing must be to put Brunow where he could do no harm. But how—where? To murder a man in cold blood was unthinkable; to keep him hidden in his room for any length of time was impossible; yet every moment he remained would be alive with deadly danger. 'Somehow or other I've got to get him into that Bristol and fly him over the lines; that's the only possible solution,' he thought swiftly, although he was by no means clear as to how he was going to get him from his room to the aeroplane. 'If I can get the machine out I'll manage it somehow or other, but I shall have to leave him here while I go down to see about it,' were the thoughts that raced through his mind.

His first action was to retrieve the revolver and slip it into his pocket. Next, he pulled the still unconscious man from under the bed, tied his hands and feet securely with a strip of towel and gagged him with a piece of the same material. Then he pushed him back far under the bed and hurried down to the tarmac, feeling that time was everything. It was nearly dark, and it could only be under cover of darkness that he could hope to get Brunow to the machine. What the mechanics would think about getting the Bristol out at such an hour he hardly knew, but there was no help for it. They could think what they liked providing they raised no objection. He found them just knocking off work, and the sergeant in charge looked at him in surprise when he asked that the two-seater be stood out on the tarmac in readiness for a flight. 'I understand I am to do some night flying soon,' Biggles told him carelessly, 'and I want some practice. Just stand her outside; there is no need for you to wait, and it may be some time before I take off. I shall be able to manage by myself.' He spoke of course in German and hoped that the N.C.O. understood what he said, but he was no means sure of it.

He breathed a sigh of relief as the mechanics obeyed his orders unquestioningly, and then disappeared in the direction of their quarters. 'All I've got to do now is to get the body there and think of a good excuse to account for my flip when I get back—if I decide to come back. Confound the fellow; what the dickens did he want to roll up here for just at this time,' he thought angrily.

He started off back towards his room, but before he reached it he saw von Stalhein hurrying along the tarmac to intercept him. 'Now what the dickens does he want, I wonder?' he muttered savagely, as the German hailed him.

'Ah, there you are,' cried von Stalhein as he came up. 'I've been looking for you. I came up to your room, but you seemed to be—well, I thought it best not to disturb you,' he smiled.

Biggles nodded. 'I had a drink or two and I must have dropped off to sleep,' he admitted.

'That's all right, but I've got a little job I want you to do for me if you will.'

'Certainly,' replied Biggles, outwardly calm but inwardly raging. 'What is it?'

'We've just had a prisoner brought in and he's as close as an oyster,' answered von Stalhein. 'He won't say a word—just sulks. We want to try the old trick on him to see if he knows anything worth knowing. Will you slip on your British uniform and we'll march you in as if you were another prisoner—you know the idea? He'll probably unloosen a bit if you start talking to him.'

'All right,' agreed Biggles, wishing that the unfortunate prisoner had chosen some other time to fall into the hands of the enemy. The trick referred to by von Stalhein was common enough. When a prisoner refused to speak, as duty demanded, and his captors thought he might be in possession of information of importance, it was customary to turn another so-called prisoner in with him, dressed in the same uniform, in the hope that confidences would be exchanged.

To Biggles this interruption of his plans at such a crucial moment was unnerving, but he could not demur, so he went to his room, and after ascertaining that Brunow was still in the position in which he had left him, he changed quickly and went along to the fort, where he found von Stalhein waiting for him with an escort of two soldiers armed with rifles and fixed bayonets.

'Where is he?' he asked.

'In the pen,' replied von Stalhein, nodding to the barbed-wire cage beside the fort in which a number of wooden huts had been erected to provide sleeping quarters.

Biggles took his place between the escort, who marched him ceremoniously to the gate of the detention camp, where another sentry was on duty. At a word of command the gate was thrown open and Biggles was marched inside. He was escorted to a room in which a light was burning. The door was unlocked; he was pushed roughly inside and the door closed behind him. But he remained standing staring unbelievably at a

British officer who sat dejectedly on a wooden stool near the far side of the room. It was Algy.

Chapter 19
Biggles Gets Busy

I

It would be hard to say who of the two was more
shaken, Biggles or Algy. For a good ten seconds they
simply stared at each other in utter amazement, and
then they both moved together. Algy sprang up and
opened his mouth to speak, but Biggles laid a warning
finger on his lips, at the same time shaking his head
violently. He covered the intervening distance in a
stride. 'Be careful—there may be dictaphones*,' he
hissed. Then aloud he exclaimed in a normal voice for
the benefit of possible listeners. 'Hello, it looks as if we
were both in the same boat. How long have you been
here?'

'They got me this afternoon,' said Algy aloud in a
disgruntled voice, but he nodded to indicate that he
grasped the reason of Biggles' warning.

'Well, it looks as if the war's over as far as we're
concerned,' continued Biggles.

'Looks like it,' agreed Algy.

Then began an amazing double-sided conversation,
one carried on in a natural way, and consisting of
such condolences and explanations as one would expect
between two British officers who found they were
brothers in misfortune. The other consisted of a whis-

---

*During the war both sides used hidden microphones, in prisoner of
war camps, to overhear the prisoners' conversation. These conversations
would be recorded on a dictaphone.

pered dialogue of why's and wherefore's, in which Biggles learnt that Algy's engine had failed and let him down in enemy country while he was flying over to Zabala with the message about the capture of El Shereef.

This went on for about half an hour, during which time Biggles racked his brains for a means of overcoming the difficulties and dangers that seemed to be closing in on him. All his original plans went by the board in the face of this new complication; first and foremost now was the pressing obsession that whatever else he did, or did not do, he must free Algy from the ghastly ordeal of spending the rest of the war in a German prison camp. What with Algy being a prisoner, Brunow tied up in his room, and von Stalhein already suspicious and waiting to spring, it can hardly be wondered at that he was appalled by the immediate prospect. One thing was certain; he must make the most of his time with Algy if ways and means of escape were to be discussed.

'I can't tell you all about it now,' he breathed, 'but things are fairly buzzing here. I don't know what's going to happen next, but I'm going to try to get you out before I do anything else; I can't tell you how exactly because I don't know myself, but I shall think of something presently. When the time comes you'll have to take your cue from me and do what you think is the right thing. For heaven's sake don't make a slip and say anything—or do anything—that will lead them to think that we know each other. I expect they'll come back in a minute to fetch me in order that I can make my report on what you've been saying, unless, of course, they've got the conversation taken down in shorthand from a dictaphone. After I've gone, stand by for anything. You come first now; I've got to get you away, and I can't worry any more about von Stalhein and his rotten schemes until that's done. In fact, this looks to me like the end of the whole business, and believe me, I shan't burst into tears if it is. I've had about enough of it. Be careful, here they come,' he went on quickly as heavy footsteps and a word of command were heard outside. 'Don't worry; I shan't be far away.'

Taking up the role he was playing, he looked over his shoulder as the door opened and the escort entered.

'Come—you,' said the N.C.O. in the harsh German military manner. He beckoned to Biggles.

Biggles rose obediently. 'Cheerio, old fellow, I may see you later perhaps,' he said casually to Algy as he left the room.

As soon as he was outside all pretence was abandoned, as of course the guards knew him, and knew quite well what was going on. The N.C.O. saluted, as did the sentry on gate duty as he left the *gefangenenlager**
and walked briskly towards the fort, thinking with the speed and clarity that is so often the result of continual flying.

Just before he reached the porch he heard an aero-engine start up and a machine begin to taxi from the Halberstadt sheds towards the far side of the aero-drome. He had a nasty moment, for at first he thought that it might be some one moving the Bristol, but he breathed again as he recognized the unmistakable purr of a Mercedes engine. He paused in his stride and a queer look came into his eyes as he peered through the darkness in the direction of the sound. 'That's the same Halberstadt going out to wait on the far side of the aerodrome, which means that friend Erich is going off

* German: prison camp.

on one of his jaunts,' he thought swiftly. For another moment or two he lingered, still thinking hard, and then he turned and walked boldly through the main porch of the fort. A light showed under the Count's door, and another under von Stalhein's, but he passed them both and went on to the far end of the corridor to what had originally been the back door of the building. He tried it and found that it was unlocked, so he went through and closed the door quietly behind him. For a moment he stood listening, and then made his way swiftly to his room where, after satisfying himself that Brunow was still unconscious, he changed into his German uniform and then hurried back to the fort. He went in by the way he had come out and emerged again through the front porch for the benefit of the sentry on duty. He did not stop but went on straight to the prison camp. 'Well, it's neck or nothing now,' he mused as he beckoned to the N.C.O. in charge of the guard. 'Bring the officer-prisoner,' he said curtly; 'Hauptmann von Stalhein wishes to speak with him.'

The N.C.O. obeyed with the blind obedience of the German soldier; he called the escort. to attention, marched them to Algy's door and called him out. Biggles did not so much as glance at him as he walked back towards the main entrance of the fort with the prisoner and his escort following.

'Wait,' he told the guards shortly, and signalling to Algy to follow, he led the way into the corridor. But he did not stop at von Stalhein's door, nor at the Count's, but went straight on to the back of the building. Little beads of perspiration were on his forehead as he opened the door and they both went outside, for he knew that if either the Count or von Stalhein had come out during the few moments they were walking through the corridor all would have been lost.

As they stepped quietly outside he looked swiftly to left and right, but no one was in sight as far as he could see, which was not very far for the moon had not yet risen. 'Come on,' he said tersely, and set off at a quick trot towards his room with Algy following close behind.

Their footfalls made no sound on the soft sand as they sprinted along the back of the hangars to the side of the building in which Biggles' room was situated. 'I daren't risk taking you in through the door in case we meet some one coming out,' he said softly, leading the way to the window. 'I had to take you through the fort to get rid of the guards,' he explained, 'but if either von Stalhein or the Count go out and see them standing there they may smell a rat, so we've no time to lose. Here we are; give me a leg up.' A jump and a heave and he was on the window-sill, reaching down for Algy, and a second later they were both standing inside the room breathing heavily from their exertion.

'Now listen,' said Biggles quietly. 'I've got a Bristol standing on the tarmac. You're going to fly it back; but you've got to take a passenger.'

'You mean—you?'

'No.'

'Who?'

'Brunow, the real Brunow. He turned up to-day.'

Algy's eyes opened wide. 'My gosh!' he breathed, 'where is he now?'

'Here.' Biggles stooped down and dragged the still unconscious man from under the bed. 'I'm afraid I socked him on the head rather hard,' he observed, 'but he asked for it. Get him to the M.O.* as soon as you can when you get back; don't for goodness' sake let him escape. Now do exactly what I tell you to,' he

* Medical Officer.

went on as he ripped off his German tunic. 'Slip this on—make haste, never mind your own tunic. If we meet any one look as much like a Hun as you can. Don't speak. I'm going to put on my overalls, but I shall be recognized so it doesn't matter much about me. Got that clear?'

'Absolutely.'

'Come on then, bear a hand; we've got to get Brunow down to the Bristol. If we are spotted I'll try to bluff that there has been an accident, but if there is an alarm follow me. I shall leave Brunow and make a dash for the machine. I'll take the pilot's seat; you get to the prop and swing it. When she starts get in as fast as you can; it would be our only chance. Are you ready?'

'Quite.'

'Then off we go. Steady—don't drop the blighter through the window, we don't want to break his neck.' Biggles looked outside, but all was silent, so between them they got the limp figure to the ground and set off at a clumsy trot towards the hangar where the British machines were housed. They reached it without seeing a soul, and to Biggles' infinite relief he saw that the Bristol was still standing as he had left it. 'We're going to have a job to get him into the cockpit,' he muttered. 'Just a minute—let me get up first.' He climbed up into the back seat, and reaching down, took Brunow by the shoulders. 'It's a good thing you got shot down to-day after all,' he panted. 'I should never have managed this job alone. He's heavier than I thought—go on—push.

Between them they got the unconscious man into the back seat and fastened the safety-belt tightly round him. 'That's fine,' muttered Biggles with satisfaction. 'If he happens to come round while you're in the air, he'll think he's dead and on the way to the place where he ought to be,' he grinned. 'Go on—in you get.'

Algy climbed into the pilot's seat while Biggles ran round to the propeller.

'Hold hard, what are you going to do?' cried Algy in sudden alarm.

'That's all right, off you go.'

'And leave you here? Not on your life.'

'Don't sit there arguing, you fool; some one will come along presently. Do as you're told.'

'Not me—not until you tell me how you're going to get back.'

'I shall probably follow you in the Pup.'

'Where is it?'

'In the hangar.'

'Can you start it alone?'

'Yes, I shall probably take straight off out of the hangar.'

'Why not get it started while I'm here?'

'I'll give you a thick ear if you don't push off,' snarled Biggles. 'I shall be all right, I tell you.'

Algy looked doubtful. 'I don't like leaving you; why not dump Brunow and let's fly back together?' he suggested.

'Because when I start on a job I like to finish it,' snapped Biggles.

'What do you mean?'

'Von Stalhein—now will you go?'

'But why—?'

'I'll shoot you if you don't start that blooming engine,' grated Biggles.

Algy saw that Biggles was in no mood to be trifled with. 'All right,' he said shortly. 'Switches off!'

'Switch off!'

'Suck in!'

'Suck in.'

Biggles pulled the big propeller round several times and then balanced it on contact. 'Contact!' he called.

'Contact!' Biggles balanced himself on the ball of his right foot and swung the blade of the propeller down. With a roar that sounded like the end of the world, the Rolls Royce engine came to life and shattered the silence with its powerful bellow.

For a minute or two Algy sat waiting for it to warm up and then looked round to wave good-bye; but Biggles had disappeared. Slowly he pushed the throttle open and the Bristol began to move over the darkened aerodrome, slowly at first but with ever increasing speed. Its tail lifted and it roared upwards into the night sky.

II

Biggles watched the Bristol take off from the inside of the hangar into which he had run for cover when the engine started. He knew that by allowing Algy to take the Bristol he had burnt his boats behind him as far as staying at Zabala was concerned, for when the prisoner was missed, and the N.C.O. in charge of the guard explained—as he was bound to—how the Engländer had been taken by Leutnant 'Brunow' to Hauptmann von Stalhein for interview, the fat would be in the fire with a vengeance. No, Zabala was finished for ever, and he knew it; all that remained for him to do was to follow the Bristol as quickly as possible into the security of the British lines.

Two methods of achieving this presented themselves, and the first was—or appeared to be—comparatively simple. It was merely to pull out the Pup, now standing in the hangar, start it up, and take off. The other made

206

a far greater appeal to him, but it was audacious in its conception and would require nerve to bring off. Curiously enough, it was while he was still weighing up the pros and cons that his mind was made up for him in no uncertain manner. It began when he walked to the back of the hangar and struck a match to see if the Pup was still in its usual position. It was, but he was staggered to see that its engine had been taken out, presumably for overhaul, and while he had not made up his mind to use the machine except in case of emergency, it gave him a shock to discover that his only safe method of escape from Zabala was effectually barred. He could have kicked himself for not finding it out earlier, for he might have based his plans on the understanding that the Pup would be airworthy. 'My word! I should have been in a bonny mess if I'd wanted it in a hurry,' he thought, and then dodged behind the wide canvas door-flap as he heard soft footsteps on the sand near at hand.

Peeping out, he saw the station *Vize-feldwebel**, who acted in the capacity of Adjutant**, standing on the tarmac looking about with a puzzled air. From his manner it was clear that he had heard the British machine take off and had hurried down to see what was going on, and Biggles blamed himself for leaving things so late, for the arrival of the *Feldwebel* was something that he had not bargained for; and he had still greater cause to regret the delay when a minute or two later the Adjutant was joined by von Stalhein. He was in a state of undress with a dressing-gown thrown over his shoulders; he, too, had evidently heard the Bristol take off and had hurried along to ascertain the cause.

* German: Sergeant Major.
** An officer specially appointed to assist the commanding officer.

He said something that Biggles did not catch to the *Feldwebel*, who went off at the double and presently returned with the Sergeant of the Flight responsible for the upkeep of the British machines—the same man to whom Biggles had given instructions regarding the preparation of the Bristol. A crisp conversation ensued, but it was carried on too quickly for Biggles to follow it, although by the mention of his name more than once, and the sergeant's actions, he guessed that the N.C.O. was explaining the reason why Leutnant Brunow was flying.

To Biggles' horror they all came into the hangar. The light was switched on, but they did not stay very long, for after von Stalhein had satisfied himself that the Bristol had actually gone, he went off and the others followed soon afterwards.

Biggles lingered no longer; the discovery of the dismantled Pup left him no choice of action, and he knew that he was faced with one of the most desperate adventures of his career, one that would either see him successful in his quest, or—but he preferred not to think of the alternative.

He was curiously calm as he stepped out of his hiding-place and set off in long swinging strides towards the far side of the aerodrome. As he walked he hummed the tune *Deutschland Über Alles* which he had often heard sung in the Mess, for the desert was forbidding in its deathly silence, and the very atmosphere seemed to be peopled by the spirits of a long-forgotten past. 'Gosh! This place gives me the creeps,' he muttered once as he stopped to get his bearings from the distant lights of Zabala, to make sure he was keeping in the right direction. 'Give me France every time.' He was far too much of a realist to be impressed by the historical associations of the ground over which he walked, land which had once been trodden by Xenophon, at the head of his gallant ten thousand, Alexander the Great, Roman generals, and Crusaders at the head of their armed hosts, but he was conscious of the vague depression that is so often the result of contact with remote antiquity. 'I don't wonder that people who get lost in the desert go dotty,' he said quietly to himself, as he quickened his pace.

He passed the bush behind which he had lain hidden on the night when he had first seen von Stalhein disguised as an Arab, and gave a little muttered exclamation of satisfaction when he saw a Halberstadt standing just where he expected to find it. Its pilot had not seen him, for he had his back towards him as he turned the propeller in the act of starting the engine. Biggles waited till the engine was ticking over and the pilot had taken his place in the front seat; then he walked up quickly, put his foot in the fuselage stirrup, swung himself up beside the pilot and tapped him on the shoulder. 'The Count wants you urgently,' he said in his best German.

'What?' exclaimed the startled pilot.

'The Count wants you,' repeated Biggles. 'There is a change of plans. I have been sent out to relieve you. Hurry up.'

'But I have been—'

'I know,' interrupted Biggles desperately, for he was afraid that von Stalhein might turn up at any moment. 'You are to go back at once. I am to fly to-night.'

To his unutterable relief the man, a rather surly fellow named Greichbach, whom he had spoken to once or twice in the Mess, made no further demur, but climbed out of his seat and stood beside the self-appointed pilot.

'What is the course to-night?' asked Biggles carelessly. 'They told me, but I had no time to write it down; I think I remember but I'd like to confirm it.'

'Jebel Hind—Galada—Wadi Baroud—Pauta,' replied the other without hesitation.

'Where do you usually land?'

'You may not have to land, but you will know in the air about that.'

'Thanks. You'd better get back now. Don't go straight across the aerodrome, though, in case I run into you taking off; go round by the boundary,' Biggles told him, and a grim smile played about the corners of his mouth as he watched the German set off in the desired direction. At the same time he released his grip on the butt of his Mauser, for the moment had been an anxious one. If was fortunate for Greichbach that he had not questioned the instructions, for Biggles had determined to have the Halberstadt even if he had to take it by force. He saw the figure of the German disappear into the darkness, still taking the course he had suggested, for the last thing he wanted to happen was for Greichbach to meet von Stalhein on the way out.

He buckled on his flying cap, pulled his goggles low over his face, removed the spare joystick from the back seat, took his place in the front cockpit, and waited. The seconds ticked by. Minutes passed and he began to feel uncomfortable, worried by the fear that Greichbach might get back to the station before von Stalhein left; but his muscles tightened with a jerk as a tall figure in Arab costume suddenly loomed up in the darkness close at hand, and without saying a word swung up into the rear cockpit.

Biggles felt a light tap on the shoulder; the word 'Go' came faintly to his ears above the noise of the engine. With a curious smile on his set face he eased the throttle open and held the stick forward. The Mercedes engine roared; the Halberstadt skimmed lightly over the sand and then soared upwards in a steep climbing turn.

Biggles saw the lights of the camp below him, and knew that whatever happened he was looking at them for the last time. Then he turned in a wide circle and, climbing slowly for height, headed for the lines.

Chapter 20
The Night Riders

I

For twenty minutes he flew on a straight course for Jebel Hind, the first landmark mentioned by Greichbach, crouching well forward in the cockpit and taking care not to turn his head to left or right, which might give von Stalhein a view of his profile. At first he could not dismiss from his mind the fear that the German would speak to him or make some move that would require an explanation, in which case exposure would be inevitable, and he wondered vaguely what von Stalhein would do about it.

As usual in two-seater aeroplanes, the pilot occupied the front seat and the observer the back one, and in this case the two cockpits were not more than a couple of feet apart. Biggles would have felt happier if the German had been in the front seat, for then he could have watched him; it was unnerving to know that an enemy whom he could not see was sitting within a couple of feet of him; but, on the other hand, he realized that if von Stalhein had been in the front seat and had happened to turn round, he would have seen him at once and discovered that a change of pilots had taken place.

'Suppose he does discover who I am, what can he do about it?' thought Biggles. 'Nothing, as far as I can see. If he hits me over the back of the head, the machine will fall and we shall both go west together, for he couldn't possibly get into my seat and take over the controls without first throwing me out; and he wouldn't have time to do that before we crashed. He'd be crazy to start a free fight in an aeroplane, anyway. The next thing is, what am *I* going to do? If he tells me to go down and land I should be able to handle the situation all right provided there isn't a party of Huns or Hun-minded Arabs waiting for him. But suppose he says nothing about landing? He'll want to know what's up if I try to land on my own account. It's no use pretending that the engine has failed, because as soon as I throttle back he'll know it by the movement of his own throttle lever. If I cut the switch and lose the engine altogether, we should probably crash trying to land, in which case I stand a better chance than he does of getting hurt. Well, we shall see.'

The lifeless rocky country around Jebel Hind loomed up ahead, and the machine bumped once or twice as the change in the terrain affected the atmosphere. The mountains of rock, heated nearly to furnace heat by the sun during the day, were not yet cool, and were throwing up columns of hot air. Cooler air from the desert was rushing in to fill the partial vacuum thus caused, and the result was vertical currents of considerable velocity.

Overcoming an almost irresistible desire to look back and see what von Stalhein was doing, he concentrated on correcting the bumps, which now became more frequent as the country below grew more rugged. A solitary searchlight stabbed a tapering finger of white light into the starry sky some little distance ahead, and he knew he was approaching the British lines. Jagged flashes of orange and crimson flame began to appear around him, showing that the anti-aircraft batteries were aware of his presence; but the searchlight had failed to pick him up and the shooting was poor, so he roared on through the night until he reached the village of Galada, when he turned sharply to the right and continued on a course that would bring him to the Wadi Baroud, which, according to Greichbach, was the next landmark.

They were flying over desert country again now, a flat expanse of wilderness surrounded on all sides by hills on which twinkled the many camp fires of troops who were being concentrated in preparation for the coming battle. 'A sort of place he might ask me to land,' thought Biggles, correcting an unusually bad bump, but the expected tap on the shoulder did not come and he roared on through the star-lit sky.

He seemed to have been flying for a long time; the cockpit was warm and cosy and his fear of the man in the back seat began to give way to lassitude. 'It's about time he was doing something,' he thought drowsily, wondering what the outcome of the whole thing would be. Strange thoughts began to drift into his mind. 'Winged chariots! Some one on the ground down there had said something about winged chariots three thousand years ago. Or was it later?' He couldn't remember, so he dismissed the matter as of no consequence, and then pulled himself up with a jerk, for he realized with a shock that he had been on the point of dozing.

The edge of the moon crept up above the rim of the desert; from his elevated position he could see it, but he knew that it was still invisible to people on the ground, which remained a vast well of mysterious darkness, broken only by vague, still darker shadows which marked the position of hills and valleys. Still he flew on, heading towards Pauta, his next landmark, which still lay some distance to the west.

Then, far ahead over his port wing appeared a little

cluster of yellow lights that he knew was the British aerodrome of Kantara; he thought for a moment, and then eased the nose of the machine a trifle towards it. Would von Stalhein notice the move and call attention to it? No, apparently not, for nothing happened. Again he touched the rudder-bar lightly and brought his nose in a straight line with the aerodrome, and almost started as a new thought flashed into his mind. 'What could he do if I decided to land there,' he mused, quivering at the idea. 'Nothing. I don't see that he could do a thing; at least, not until we were actually on the ground. Then he'd probably try to pull a gun on me, jump into the pilot's seat and escape. Well, I can act as quickly as he can,' he thought. The more he toyed with the plan the more it appealed to him. It would end the whole business one way or the other right away. To march the German up to Major Raymond's tent would be a fitting end to his adventures. Von Stalhein's plans, whatever they were, would not— could not—materialize then. But whatever he did would have to be done quickly. 'The moment I start to glide down he'll know something's wrong, and he'll be on his feet in a jiffy,' he thought. 'And then anything can happen. No! When I go down I'll go so fast that he won't be able to speak, move, or do anything else except hang on. Maybe he'll think that something has broken and we're falling out of control; so much the better if he does.'

Tingling with excitement, he held on to his course, watching the aerodrome lights creeping slowly nearer. They were nearly under the leading edge of his port wing now—still nearer they crept—nearer. Suddenly they disappeared from sight and he knew he was over the middle of the aerodrome. A glance at the luminous altimeter showed the needle resting on the five-thou-

215

sand-feet mark. It was now or never. 'Well, come on,' he muttered aloud, and did several things simultaneously. With his left hand he cut the throttle; his left foot kicked the rudder-bar, while with his right hand he flung the joystick over to the left and then dragged it back into his right thigh.

To any one in the back seat, experienced or otherwise, the result would have been terrifying—as indeed he intended it to be. The machine lurched drunkenly as it quivered in a stall; its nose flopped over heavily, swung down, and then plunged earthward in a vicious spin. With his eyes glued on the whirling cluster of lights below, Biggles counted the revolutions dispassionately. When he reached number five he shoved the stick forward, kicked on top rudder, and then spun in the opposite direction. At what he judged to be trifle less than a thousand feet he pulled out of the spin, and then pushed his left wing down in a vertical side-slip. A blast of air struck him on the side of the face, while struts and wires howled in protest—but still the machine dropped like a stone.

Only at the last moment did he level out, make a swift S turn and glide in to a fast wheel landing. As his wheels touched the ground he flicked off the ignition switch with a sharp movement of his left hand while with his right he felt for the Mauser. The tail-skid dropped, dragged a few yards, and the machine stopped. Biggles made a flying leap at the ground, revolver in hand.

'Stick up your hands, von Stalhein,' he snapped.

There was no reply.

'Come on, stick 'em up; I've got you covered. One false move and it's your last—I mean it.'

Still no reply.

Biggles stooped low so that he could see the sil-

216

houette of the cockpit against the sky, but he could not see the German. 'Come on, look lively,' he snarled. 'It's no use crouching down there on the floor. In five seconds I shall start shooting.'

Still no reply.

Biggles felt a thrill of doubt run through him. Had von Stalhein jumped out, too? He dodged round to the far side of the machine and looked around; he could see a hundred yards in all directions, but there was no one in sight. With his revolver ready, he put his foot in the fuselage stirrup and stood up so that he could see inside the back cockpit. One glance was enough. It was empty.

He put the gun back into his pocket and leaned weakly against the trailing edge of the lower wing. 'I'm mad,' he muttered, 'daft—dreaming. I've got sun-stroke—that's what it is.' He closed his eyes, shook his head violently, and then opened them again. 'No, it isn't a dream,' he went on, as he saw mechanics racing towards the spot. The reaction after the terrific strain of the last few minutes, when every nerve had been keyed up to breaking-point, was almost overwhelming. The unexpected anti-climax nearly upset his mental balance. He threw back his head and laughed aloud.

'Hands up, there, Jerry!' yelled the leading mechanic as he ran up.

'What are you getting excited about?' snarled Biggles.

The shock to the unfortunate ack emma* when he heard a normal English voice was nearly as great as Biggles' had been a few moments before. He stared at the pilot, then at the machine, and then back at Biggles.

A flight-sergeant pushed his way to the front of the

* Slang: Aircraft Mechanic.

217

rapidly forming group of spectators. 'What's all this?' he growled.

'It's all right; I've brought you a souvenir, flight-sergeant,' grinned Biggles, indicating the machine with a nod. 'You can take it, you can keep it, and you can jolly well stick it up your tunic as far as I'm concerned. And I hope it bites you,' he added bitterly, as he realized that his well-laid plans, carried out at frightful risk, had come to naught.

'Any one else in that machine?' asked the flight-sergeant suspiciously.

'Take a look and see,' invited Biggles. 'As a matter of fact there is, but I can't find him. Just see if you can do any better.'

The flight-sergeant made a swift examination of the Halberstadt. 'No, sir, there's nobody here,' he said.

'That's what I thought,' murmured Biggles slowly.

The flight-sergeant eyed him oddly, and then looked relieved when a number of officers, who had heard the machine land, ran up and relieved him of any further responsibility in the matter. Major Raymond was amongst them, and Biggles took him gently by the arm. 'Better get the machine in a hangar out of the way, sir,' he said. 'If people start asking questions I shall tell them that I'm a delivery pilot taking a captured machine down to the repair depot, but I lost my way and had to make a night landing. I'll wait for you in your tent. Is Algy back?'

'Yes; he was in the Mess having his dinner when I came out. He said something about not letting stray Huns interfere with his meals.'

'He wouldn't,' replied Biggles bitterly. 'Has he told you—'

'Yes, he's told me all about it.'

'And Brunow?'

The Major nodded. 'Yes, we've got him where he can do no harm. You'd better trot along to the Mess and get something to eat, and then come and see me in my tent.'

'Right you are, sir.' Biggles started off in the direction of the distant Officers' Mess.

II

An hour later he reclined in a long cane chair in Major Raymond's tent. The Major sat at his desk with his chin resting in the palms of his hands; Algy sat on the other side of him, listening.

'Well, there it is,' Biggles was saying. 'I think it was, without exception, the biggest shock I have ever had in my life—and I've had some, as you know. It was also the biggest disappointment. I'll tell you straight, sir. I could have burst into tears when I landed and found he wasn't there. I couldn't believe it, and that's a fact. When I think of all the trouble I went to, and risks I took—but there, what's the use of moaning about it? I only hope he broke his blinking neck on a perishing boulder when he hit the floor.'

'How do you mean?'

'Well, there's no doubt about what he did. When he was over the place where he wanted to get to he just stepped over the side with a parachute; there's no other solution that I can think of—unless, of course, he suddenly got tired of life and took a running jump into space. Or he may have decided to go for a stroll, forgetting where he was, but knowing von Stalhein pretty well I should say that's hardly likely. No! the cunning blighter stepped over with a brolley, and I can guess where it happened. I remember an extra bad bump. And for all I know he's been getting into our lines like

219

that all the time. After all, it's no more risky than landing in an aeroplane in a rough country like this. The point is he's still alive and kicking, and from my point of view, the sooner he makes his last kick the better. He's not a man; he's a rattlesnake. He's somewhere over this side of the lines floating about in his Ali Baba outfit. How are we going to find him?—that's what I want to know. By the way, Algy, how did you get on with Brunow?'

'Right as rain, no trouble at all. I flew straight back and landed here. I dumped him in my room with a sentry on guard, slipped an overcoat over my Hun uniform, and reported to the Major. Brunow came round just as I got back and took off my coat. He started bleating a prayer of thanksgiving when he saw my uniform, and then told me in no uncertain terms just what sort of swine the British were and what he thought of you in particular. He asked me if you'd been arrested yet, and if so, when were you to be shot.'

'Go on,' put in Biggles interestedly. 'What did you tell him?'

'I just broke the news gently, and told him he'd got things all wrong. He wouldn't believe it at first, and I had to explain that since the last time he was awake he'd been on a long, long journey, and was now nicely settled in the hands of the British swines.'

'What did he say to that?'

'He didn't say anything; he just went all to pieces. Now he's trying to pretend that he didn't mean it.'

'Where is he now?'

'In the Kantara prison camp, in solitary confinement,' put in the Major.

'What are you going to do with him, sir?'

'He'll be tried by General Court Martial, of course.

But what about this fellow von Stalhein? That's far more important.'

'I was coming to that,' answered Biggles slowly. 'I think we can lay him by the heels, but I shall want some help.'

'What sort of help?'

'Personal assistance from somebody who knows the country well—and the Arabs; Major Sterne for instance.'

Major Raymond looked serious. 'He's a difficult fellow to get hold of,' he said. 'He's all over the place, and we seldom know just where he is. Won't any one else do?'

'I'd prefer Sterne. It's only right that as he caught El Shereef, he should have a hand in the affair. Surely if you sent out an SOS amongst the Arabs it would reach his ears and he'd come in.'

'He might. He doesn't like being interfered with when he's on a job, but if the matter was exceptionally serious he might take it the right way. Just what do you suggest?'

'I suggest that a message be sent out that his presence is urgently required at General Headquarters in connexion with plans for the British advance, so will he please report as quickly as possible. That should bring him in.'

'But good gracious, man, the General would never consent to that.'

'Why not? He more than any one else should be glad to lay a dangerous fellow like von Stalhein by the heels.'

'And suppose I can arrange it: where would you like to see Sterne?'

'At General Headquarters, if possible; it would save him coming here. If you'll get the message out I'll go to headquarters with Lacey and wait until he comes. Perhaps you'd like to come along too?'

'The General isn't going to be pleased if you waste his time.'

'I shan't be pleased if I waste my own, if it comes to that,' observed Biggles coolly. 'I've been risking my neck, so he can hardly object to giving up a few minutes of his time. All right, sir, let's start moving.'

Chapter 21
Sterne Takes a Hand

The pearly glow of a new day spread slowly over the eastern sky; it threw a cold grey light over the inhospitable wilderness, and intensified the whiteness of a house that stood on the outskirts of the village of Jebel Zaloud, a house that once had been the residence of the merchant Ali Ben Sadoum, but was now the air Headquarters of the British Expeditionary Force in Palestine.

A wan beam crept through the unglazed window of a room on the ground floor, and awoke two officers who were sleeping uncomfortably in deck chairs. Biggles started, blinked, and then sprang to his feet as he observed the daylight. 'Looks as if he isn't coming, Algy,' he said crisply. 'It's getting light.'

Algy rubbed his eyes, yawned, and stood up, stretching. 'You're right,' he said. 'In which case we shall have to try to find the wily Erich ourselves, I suppose.'

'Yes; it's a pity though,' muttered Biggles thoughtfully, rubbing his chin. 'I hoped we should save ourselves a lot of trouble.' He yawned. 'We must have dropped off to sleep soon after midnight. Well, well, it can't be helped, but I expect the General will be peeved if he's been waiting about all night.'

'He wasn't going to bed anyway,' Algy told him. 'I heard the Brigade-Major say that the General would be up most of the night working on important dispatches. Where is Raymond do you suppose?'

'Up in the General's room, I imagine—he was last night.'

'Gosh! he'll be sick if we let the General down.'

'I expect he will; as I said before, it's a pity, but it can't be helped. I've acted as I thought best.'

There was a tap on the door and an orderly appeared. 'The General wishes to see you in his room immediately,' he said.

Biggles grimaced. 'This is where we get our ears twisted,' he muttered ruefully, as he followed the orderly to a large apartment on the first floor.

The General looked up wearily from his desk as they entered. Several Staff officers and Major Raymond were there, and they regarded the two airmen with disapproval plainly written on their faces.

'Which of you is Bigglesworth?' began the General.

Biggles stepped forward. 'I am, sir,' he said.

'Will you have the goodness to explain what all this means? Major Raymond has told me of the excellent work you have done since you have been in Palestine, and in view of that I am prepared to take a broad view, but I am very tired, and this business all seems very pointless.'

Biggles looked uncomfortable. 'I agree, sir, it does,' he admitted; 'but I had hoped to prove that my unusual request was justified.'

'I believe it was on your intervention that stay of execution was granted in the death sentence promulgated in connexion with Sheikh Haroun Ibn Said, otherwise the spy, El Shereef. Frankly, Bigglesworth, we are prepared to give officers sent out here on special detached duty from the Air Board a lot of rope, but there is a limit as to how far we can allow them to interfere with ordinary service routine.'

224

'Quite, sir. I hope to repay you for your consideration.'

'How?'

'By saving you from the mental discomfort you would surely have suffered when you discovered that you had shot an innocent man, sir.'

'Innocent man! What are you talking about?'

'The Sheikh Haroun Ibn Said is not El Shereef, sir.' Biggles spoke quietly but firmly.

'Good heavens, man, what do you mean?'

'What I say, sir. The whole thing was a frame-up— if I may use an American expression. Sheikh Haroun is what he has always claimed to be—a good friend of the British. By causing him to be arrested and—as they hoped—shot as a spy, the German agent who handled the job hoped to achieve two ends. To remove a powerful Sheikh who was sincerely loyal to British arms, and at the same time lull you into a sense of false security by leading you to believe that you had at last put an end to the notorious activities of the spy, El Shereef. Sheikh Haroun Ibn Said, in his ignorance of western matters, was easily induced to wear a German Secret Service ring, and carry on his person incriminating documents without having the slightest idea of what they meant. In short, he was induced to adopt the personality of El Shereef.'

The General's face was grim. 'By whom?' he snapped.

'By El Shereef, sir,' said Biggles simply.

The General started and a look of understanding dawned in his eyes. Silence fell on the room. What Biggles had just told him might not have occurred to him, but its dreadful possibilities were now only too apparent. 'Good God!' he breathed. 'Are you sure of this?'

225

'I am, sir.'

'So El Shereef is still at large.'

'He is, sir.'

'Who is the man whom you flew into the British lines last night—Major Raymond has told me about it—this Hauptmann Erich von Stalhein. Has he any connexion with El Shereef?'

'He has, sir.'

'What is it?'

'He's the same man, sir—El Shereef.'

Another silence fell. The General sat staring like a man hypnotized, and so did his staff for that matter, although one or two of them looked incredulous.

'Why did you not tell me this before?' asked the General harshly. There was reproach and anger in his voice.

'Because there was a thing that I valued above all others at stake, sir,' replied Biggles firmly. 'For that reason I told nobody what I had discovered.'

'And what was that?'

'My life, sir. I do not mean to be disrespectful, but German agents have ears in the very highest places— even in your headquarters, sir.'

The General frowned. 'I find it hard to believe that,' he said. 'Still, this story of yours puts a very different complexion on things. Von Stalhein, alias El Shereef, is still at large, and you want Sterne to help you run him to earth—is that it?'

'That is correct, sir.'

'I see. I sent out a general call for him last night, but it begins to look as if he isn't coming. If he does come, I'll let you know.'

There was a sharp rap on the door, and the duty Staff sergeant entered. 'Major Sterne is here, sir,' he said.

'Ask him to come up here at once,' ordered the General. 'I'll speak to him first and tell him what is proposed,' he added quickly, turning to Biggles.

'Thank you, sir.' Biggles, after a nod to Algy, stepped back against the far wall.

The next moment he was watching with a kind of fascinated interest a man who had swept into the room, for he knew he was looking at one of the most talked-of men in the Middle East, a man whose knowledge of native law was proverbial and who could disguise himself to deceive even the Arabs themselves. Even now he was dressed in flowing Arab robes, but he clicked his heels and raised his hand in the military salute.

'Hello, Sterne, here you are then,' began the General, as he reached over his desk and shook hands. 'You got my message?'

'Yes, sir,' replied the other briskly. 'I was anxious to know what it was about.'

'It's about this confounded fellow, El Shereef,' continued the General. 'It seems that there has been some mistake; the fellow you brought in was not El Shereef at all.'

Biggles stepped forward quietly.

'Not El Shereef!' cried Sterne. 'What nonsense! If *he* isn't El Shereef, then who is?'

'You are, I think,' said Biggles quietly. 'Don't move—von Stalhein.'

The man who had been known as Major Sterne spun round on his heel and looked into the muzzle of Biggles' revolver. He lifted eyes that were glittering with hate to Biggles' face. 'Ah,' he said softly, and then again, 'Ah. So I was right.'

'You were,' said Biggles shortly, 'and so was I.'

Von Stalhein slowly raised his hands. As they drew level with the top of his burnous, he tore the garment

227

off with a swift movement and hurled it straight into Biggles' face. At the same time he leapt for the door. Algy barred his way, but he turned like a hare and sprang at the window with Algy at his heels. For a second pandemonium reigned.

Biggles dared not risk shooting for fear of hitting Algy or the Staff officers who tried to intercept the German; but they were too late. Biggles saw a flash of white as von Stalhein went through the window like a bird. He did not attempt to follow, but dashed through the door, shouting for the headquarter's guard. 'Outside, outside,' he shouted furiously, as they came running up the stairs. He dashed past them, raced to the door, and looked out. An Arab, bent double over a magnificent horse, was streaking through the village street. Before Biggles could raise his weapon horse and rider had disappeared round the corner of the road that led to Kantara.

'Get my car, get my car,' roared the General. 'Baines! Baines! Where the devil are you? Confound the man, he's never here when he's wanted.'

'Here, sir.' The chauffeur, very red about the ears, for he had been snatching a surreptitious cup of tea with the cook, started the big Crossley tourer and took his place at the wheel.

The General jumped in beside him, and the others squeezed into the back seats. There was not room for Algy, but determined not to be left behind, he flung himself on the running board.

'Faster, man, faster,' cried the General, as they tore through the village with Arabs, mangy dogs, scraggy fowls, and stray donkeys missing death by inches. The car, swaying under its heavy load, dry-skidded round the corner where von Stalhein had last been seen, and the open road lay before them.

A mile away the tents of Kantara gleamed pink and gold in the rays of the rising sun; two hundred yards this side of them von Stalhein was flogging his horse unmercifully, as, crouching low in the saddle, he sped like an arrow towards the hangars.

'He'll beat us,' fumed the General. 'He'll take one of those machines just starting up.'

It was apparent that such was von Stalhein's intention. Several machines of different types were standing on the tarmac; the propeller of one of them, a Bristol Fighter, was flashing in the sunlight, warming up the engine while its pilot and observer finished their cigarettes outside the Mess some thirty or forty yards away.

Von Stalhein swerved like a greyhound towards the machine. The pilot and observer watched his unusual actions in astonishment; they made no attempt to stop him.

At a distance of ten yards von Stalhein pulled up with a jerk that threw the horse on to its haunches; in a twinkling of an eye he had pulled away the chocks from under the wheels and had taken a flying leap into the cockpit. The engine roared and the Bristol began to move over the ground.

'We've lost him,' cried the General. Then, as an afterthought, he added, 'Stop at the archie battery, Baines.'

The usual protective anti-aircraft battery was only a hundred yards down the road, the muzzles of its four guns pointing into the air like chimneys set awry as the crews sleepily sipped their early morning tea. But the arrival of the General's car brought them to their feet with a rush. A startled subaltern ran forward and saluted.

'Get that machine,' snapped the General, pointing at the Bristol that was now a thousand feet in the air

229

and climbing swiftly towards the German lines. 'Get it and I'll promote you to Captain in to-night's orders.'

The lieutenant asked no questions; he shouted an order and dashed to the range-finder. Mess tins were flung aside as the gunners leapt to their stations, and within five seconds the first gun had roared its brass-coated shell at the British machine. It went wide. The officer corrected the aim, and a second shot was nearer. Another correction, and a shell burst fifty yards in front of the two-seater. Another word of command, and the four guns began firing salvoes as fast as the gunners could feed them.

Tiny sparks of yellow flame, followed by mushrooming clouds of white smoke, appeared round the Bristol, the pilot of which began to swerve from side to side as he realized his danger.

Biggles was torn between desire to watch the frantic but methodical activity of the gunners—for he had seldom stood at the starting end of archie—and the machine, but he could not tear his eyes away from the swerving two-seater; knowing from bitter experience just what von Stalhein was going through, he felt almost sorry for him. A shell burst almost under the fuselage and the machine rocked.

'He's hit,' cried the General excitedly.

'No, sir, it was only the bump of the explosion, I think,' declared Biggles.

Another shell burst almost between the wings of the Bristol, and its nose jerked up spasmodically.

'He's hit now, sir,' yelled Biggles, clutching Algy's arm.

A silence fell on the little group of watchers; the roar of the guns and the distant sullen *whoof—whoof—whoof* of the bursting shells died away as the Bristol lurched, recovered, lurched again, and then fell off on its wing into a dizzy earthward plunge. Twice it tried to come out, as if the pilot was still alive and making desperate efforts to right his machine; then it disappeared behind a distant hill.

A hush of tense expectancy fell as every man held his breath and strained his ears for the sound that he knew would come.

It came. Clear-cut through the still morning air, far away over the German side of the lines, came the sound as if some one had jumped on a flimsy wooden box, crushing it flat: the sinister but unmistakable sound of an aeroplane hitting the ground.

Biggles drew a deep breath. 'Well,' he said slowly, 'that's that.'

Chapter 22
Biggles Explains

That evening a little party dined quietly in the Head-quarters Mess; it consisted of the General, his Aide-de-Camp, Major Raymond, Algy, and Biggles, who, over coffee, at the General's request, ran over the whole story.

'And so you see, sir,' he concluded, 'the unravelling of the skein was not so difficult as one might imagine.'

'But when did you first suspect that von Stalhein and El Shereef were one and the same?' asked the General.

'It's rather hard to say, sir,' replied Biggles slowly. 'I fancy the idea was at the back of my mind before I was really aware of it—if I can put it that way,' he continued. 'I felt from the very beginning that von Stalhein was more than he appeared to be on the surface.'

'Why did you think that?'

'Because he was so obviously suspicious—not only where I was concerned but with any stranger that came to the camp. "Why should he be?" I asked myself, and the only answer I could find was, because he had more to lose than any one else on the station. After all, a man is only suspicious when he has something to be suspicious about. Something was going on behind the scenes. What was it? When I saw him dressed as an Arab—well, that seemed to be the answer to the question.

'He never appeared in that garb in daylight, and I

am convinced that only a few people at Zabala knew what he was doing; he didn't want them to know; that's why he used to send the aeroplane to the far side of the aerodrome and slip out after dark when no one was about. The Count knew all about it, of course; he had to, and if you ask my opinion I should say that he wasn't too pleased about it—hence his attitude towards me.'

'But why should he feel like that?'

'Because he was secretly jealous of von Stalhein. He wanted all the kudos. Von Faubourg was vain and inefficient and it annoyed him to know that a subordinate had ten times the amount of brain that he had; he had sense enough to recognize that, you may be sure. And von Stalhein knew it too. He knew that nothing would please the Count more than to see him take down a peg. I will go as far as to say that I believe the Count was actually pleased when von Stalhein's plans went wrong. Take the business of the Australian troops, for example. Von Stalhein put that over to try to trap me; he merely wanted to see what I would do in such a case. When I got back and reported that the Australians were at Sidi Arish the Count was tickled to death because von Stalhein's scheme had failed; I could tell it by his manner. He was so pleased that he came round to my room to congratulate me. That showed me how things were between them, and I knew that I had a friend in the Count as long as I didn't tread on his toes; the more I upset von Stalhein—to a point—the better he was pleased.

'Take the business of when I dropped my ring near the waterworks. That was a careless blunder that might have cost me my life; even the Count couldn't overlook that, but he was quite pleased when I cleared myself for no other reason than that von Stalhein had told

233

him that he had got me stone cold. If the Count had made the discovery it would have been quite a different matter. Von Stalhein sent Leffens out to watch me. Leffens was, I think, the one man he really trusted; he used to fly him over the lines until I killed him, and after that he used Mayer. He never knew what happened to Leffens, but he thought he did when he found one of his bullets in my machine. I've got a feeling that he tipped Leffens off to shoot me down if he got a chance, and that was why he daren't make much of a song when he found the bullet.

'I had already thought a lot about Sterne, who as far as I could make out was playing pretty much the same game for the British, and there were two things that put me on the right track there. First, the shadow on the tent, and secondly, the fact that some one—obviously in sympathy with the Germans—arranged my escape. Who could it be? Who had access to British posts? Mind you, sir, at that stage the association was nothing more than a bare possibility. I could hardly bring myself to believe that it might be remotely possible, but once the germ was in my mind it stayed there, and I was always on the look-out for a clue that might confirm it. That's why I went to von Stalhein's room. I hardly admitted it to myself but I knew I was hoping to find a British uniform—or something of the sort. As a matter of fact I did see a Sam Browne belt in the wardrobe, but I could hardly regard that as proof; it might easily have been nothing more than a souvenir. But then there was the British hat in Mayer's machine! It may sound easy to put two and two together now but it wasn't so easy then. Would you have believed me, sir, if I had come to you and said that Major Sterne was von Stalhein? I doubt it.

'Von Stalhein's scheme for the capture of El Shereef

was a clever piece of work, there's no denying that; it shook me to the marrow. At first it took me in, and I'll admit it. But he overreached himself. He made one little slip—took one risk, would perhaps be nearer the truth—and it gave the game away. Then I saw how simple the whole thing really was.'

'Do you mean when you went and saw Sheikh Haroun?' put in the Major.

'No, I got nothing out of him,' declared Biggles. 'He behaved just as one would expect a well-bred Arab to behave in such circumstances. He closed up like an oyster at the bare thought of the British suspecting him to be a traitor, and he would have died with his mouth shut if I hadn't butted in. No, it was what I saw in your tent that gave the game away.'

'What was it?'

'The ring. Those rings are few and far between. They daren't leave spare ones lying about: it would be too dangerous. Yet they knew that one of those rings found on the Sheikh would be sufficient evidence to hang him. There was only one available; it was Leffens', and I recognized it—as, indeed, I had every reason to. That set me thinking, and I reconstructed the crime—as the police say. Yet I had to act warily. One word and we shouldn't have seen von Stalhein—El Shereef—call him what you like—for dust and small pebbles.'

'But he sent you over to try to rescue El Shereef,' exclaimed the General. 'What was his idea in doing that?'

'It was simply another try-on; he wanted me to confirm that El Shereef had been arrested, and at the same time he hoped I'd make a boob. He had nothing to lose. Suppose I had managed to "rescue" El Shereef—or rather, Sheikh Haroun. The Huns would have asked for nothing more than to have had him in their hands.'

235

'Yes, of course, I quite see that. And by reporting that he had been shot you led him to think that we had been completely taken in.'

'Exactly, sir. I went on playing my own game, and as it happened it came off, although he made a clever move to get rid of me. He never trusted me; he was no fool; he was the only one of the lot of them who spotted that things started going wrong from the moment I arrived. It might have been coincidence, but von Stalhein didn't think so.'

'How do you mean?'

'Well, first of all the waterworks were blown up; then Leffens failed to return; then the Arab raid went wrong; then Hess got killed! Mayer crashes and gets his leg smashed—oh, no, sir, he wasn't going to believe this was just a run of bad luck. Something was radically wrong somewhere and he knew it. Whether it was anything to do with me or not, he would have felt happier if he could have got me out of the way. That's why he tried to get me pushed into the ground.'

'When?'

'The day I came over here to confirm that you had captured El Shereef.'

'What did he do?'

'He followed me over in the Pup—dressed as Major Sterne. He simply walked along the tarmac, told the flight-sergeant to put my machine in the shed and put another in its place—one which, of course, had no distinguishing mark on the top plane.'

'You assume he did that?'

'I assumed it at the time; I know it now.'

'How?'

'I've asked the flight-sergeant about it and he told me just what happened; he obeyed the Major's orders unquestioningly, as he was bound to. Then von Stalhein went back and sent out the Pfalz crowd to intercept me on the way home. It was clever, that, because if I had been shot no one would have been the wiser. I should just have disappeared, and that was all he wanted. But I knew things were rapidly coming to a head, and that's why I played a big stake to end it one way or the other; but all the same, I thought I'd bungled things badly when I landed here and found he wasn't in the back seat of that Halberstadt. I never even thought of his going over the side by parachute. After that there was one chance left, for if once a hue and cry had started we should never have seen him again, you may be sure of that. Von Stalhein had set plenty of traps, so I thought it was about time I set one, with what result you know.'

'And what do you propose to do now?' asked the General.

'I am going to submit an application to you, sir, to post me back to my old unit, number 266 Squadron in France, and I hope you will put it through, sir.'

The General looked hurt. 'I hoped you would stay out here,' he said. 'I could have found you a place on Headquarters Staff—both of you.'

'I'm sorry, sir—it's very kind of you—but—well, somehow I don't feel at home here. I would prefer to go back to France if you have no objection.'

'Very well, so be it. I can't refuse, and I need hardly say how grateful I am for what you have done during your tour of duty in the Middle East. The success of the British Army in Palestine may have rested on you alone. Naturally, I am forwarding a report on your work to the Air Board, and doubtless they will ask you to do the same. And now I must get back to my work— pray that you are never a General, Bigglesworth.'

'I should think that's the last thing I'm ever likely

237

to be, sir,' smiled Biggles. 'A Camel, blue skies, and plenty of Huns is the height of my ambition, and I hope to find them all in France. Good-bye, sir.'

'Good-bye—and good luck.' The General watched them go and then turned to his Aide-de-Camp. 'If we had a few more officers of that type the war would have been over long ago,' he observed.